THE GARRISON PROJECT

DAVID J. THIRTEEN

BAD LUCK
BOOKS

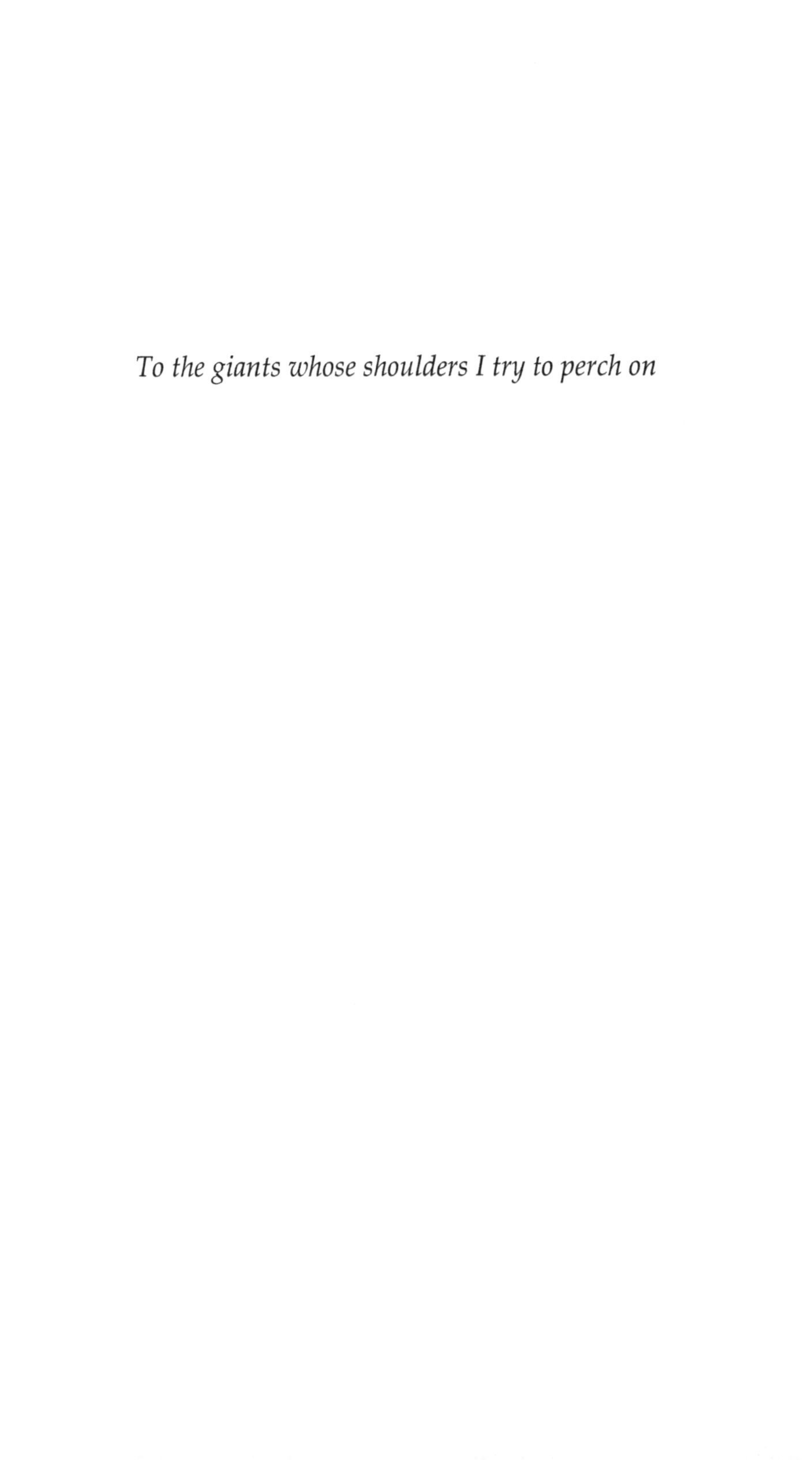

To the giants whose shoulders I try to perch on

1.

LIKE A DISEASE, stories spread. Urban legends were simply another type of infection. They jumped from person to person, corrupting everyone they touched. Along the way, they changed, mutated, becoming more virulent with each new strain.

When a story was told, it was never clear how far it had traveled or how many hosts it had passed through. That night, many tales made their way around the dinner table to challenge Molly, but none of them were new to her. She knew their history and their etymology. Just as an epidemiologist would have listened to a list of symptoms, Molly stayed detached from the lurid nature of the tales. Her head nodded and a bored but polite smile played on her lips as she picked apart each speaker's unique additions and flourishes.

She had heard them all. Except for the last one.

"If you don't believe me, I'll show you." In his haste to retrieve the phone from his pocket, Keith slammed his wine down. The Chianti rolled across the balloon of the glass in a burgundy tempest that threatened to spill over.

Charlotte scolded him. "No phones. You know I hate it when people take those things out in a restaurant."

It was Friday night and they were at the same neighborhood joint the eight of them used to meet at when they attended college together. It was a kitschy Italian place that hadn't changed in decades. It had the same red-and-white checkered tablecloths and wicker wrapped wine bottles that had been on display since before any of them were born.

Being together again brought with it a strange nostalgia that was both joyous and depressing. So many good memories were bubbling just beneath the surface, Molly had the giddy feeling she'd stepped back in time. But this reunion was also a stark reminder that unlike her friends, who had moved on with careers, families, and "real life," she was still treading water at Milton College. It was almost as though she was a remnant from those memories of the good old days — nothing but a ghost invoked by this séance of wine and pasta.

Kevin, her dear Kevin, leaned forward putting his sleeve in the scattered crumbs left behind on the cloth. He gave that wry smile of his, the one that caused his dimple to come out and signaled he was about to launch a devastating argument. "Watching it wouldn't change anything. I'm not going to believe a video you found on the Internet. I've seen what a high-school kid with a laptop can do. Nowadays, faking a haunting is easier than putting two holes in a sheet."

"That's what makes this weird. Nothing supernatural happens on the tape, but it's insanely creepy." Keith grabbed the last cannoli and nibbled the cream filling off the end. "It starts like this hokey home renovation show. Then they tear down a wall and…bam! Behind it is all this freaky occult stuff. It gave me chills, I tell you. You really have to see it."

Molly asked, "If that's all it is, why did you say the house was haunted?"

"From the website. It explained what happened to the family. After they tore the wall down, they suffered all kinds of problems. Someone falls off the roof, there's a power tool accident, that sort of stuff. All because they released a spirit when they opened up that wall."

"Then what happens?"

"I guess they moved. Wouldn't you?" Keith brushed icing sugar from his mustache. "If it were me, I would've moved the second I found any satanic shit."

"If it were you," Charlotte said, "the guy's wife would still be waiting for the wall to get torn down. Home improvements — the horror, the horror." She placed her hands to her cheeks in a mocking impression of Munch's *Scream*.

The discussion devolved into laughter while Keith finished his second helping of dessert and pretended to ignore the jokes at his expense.

Molly didn't realize there had been any tension in the air until her laugh burst out of her. Or maybe the tension hadn't been in the air at all. Maybe it only existed as an inner clenching, a tightening at her core as the possibilities of this story drew her in.

It was exactly the sort of thing she had been looking for: a mundane occurrence that becomes a supernatural tale in the telling. Someone posts footage with something a little strange in it. Someone else elaborates by adding on a string of tragedies. Then at a dinner party, it gets brought up as a ghost story. If Molly weren't writing her master's thesis on urban myths, would she now tell a friend over lunch about this family plagued by a poltergeist, even though she never knew them and never saw the video? Would she add her own little touches, having forgotten some of the details Keith had mentioned? Would her friend then go out into the world to create the next slightly different version?

This was how they spread. Could she catch this story so close to its origin?

On a sunny morning two days later, Molly sat at her desk by the window overlooking the spires and rooftops of the sleepy New England town. In her inbox, was a message from Keith. It only contained a link. When she clicked on it, a new window opened on her computer screen and the video began to play.

DAY 3: DEMOLITION

IT'S OBVIOUS FROM THE START this video was not created by professionals. The graphic at the opening is nothing but a basic in-camera title card, with the heading "The Garrison Project," and the name of the episode.

A man in a denim shirt adjusts the camera angle while staring into the lens. He looks to be in his late twenties. His jaw is square and he has clear, hypnotic blue eyes. He's attractive enough to be an actor. So is the woman behind him.

Once he's satisfied with the positioning, he retreats to her keeping his hand stretched out as though afraid the camera will fall without his constant touch.

The woman is petite — more than a head shorter than him. And despite the oversized work gloves and bandana she wears, she's striking. A stray curl of dark hair escapes her do-rag and outlines her pronounced cheekbone. Her face is without blemish and her skin has a healthy tan.

Any suspicion this might be scripted or fake is dispelled as they launch into their introduction and prove themselves to be awkward and stiff in front of the camera. "Hi. This is Charlie Garrison," he says.

"And this is Mary Garrison," she says.

"And welcome to our new home. In our last episode, I…we took you on the grand tour. Today we're going to be opening up this wall behind us."

"Goodbye, wall," Mary says, smiling and patting the plastered surface. "Can't wait to be rid of you."

"We've had the engineer in and he's confirmed it's not loadbearing. So we're going ahead with our plans to combine the dining room and the den into one."

"We can't even fit our table and chairs in here now, but once we steal the space from the den, we're going to have a fabulous place to entertain. And as an added bonus, it will improve the whole flow of the house."

"That's right." Charlie pauses and for a second it's as though he's forgotten what he was about to say, but he recovers with a stammer. "Right now, this wall blocks the flow and we have to walk all the way through the house to get to the dining room." He diagrams a semicircle on his palm for the viewer to see. "With it gone, we'll be able to reach it from the entry hall too." His index finger makes a full loop on his hand.

"Foyer," Mary corrects, drawing out the last syllable and rolling it for emphasis. "It's a foyer."

Small children argue in the background. Their words are indistinct and crackle. It could be nothing but a stray radio signal breaking through on the audio frequency, until a shrill voice screams, "Stop it. Stop it. It's mine."

"Henry, leave your brother alone." A person behind the camera and off to the right draws Charlie's attention. "No, don't come in here. It's too dangerous. Play at the table until we're done. What did I say? Stay in the kitchen." He marches out of frame to intercept Henry. Whatever occurs between father and son is lost as the image skips in the first and only edit of the broadcast.

After the flicker of missing footage, both Mary and Charlie are on screen but the camera has been repositioned to focus on the corner. The room's small window shows raindrops and the siding of the neighbor's house. Mary is preparing to make her first swing with the sledgehammer. She pumps it back and forth like a batter warming up but lacks the strength to keep it level. By the fourth practice swing, the weight has dragged it down to the angle of a golf club. Mary lets loose and a chunk of plaster the size of a dinner plate comes off and crumbles to the floor, while a spiderweb of cracks spread out over the dull white surface.

She takes three more whacks at it, but doesn't manage to break through the wooden slats. Plaster dust settles on the camera lens, fogging the scene.

"Here. I'll take over," Charlie says.

She holds the hammer out to him and backs away.

"Let me show you how it's done." He hauls back and lets the hammer fly, only for it to bounce off the wall. The recoil sends him stumbling to one knee.

Out of shot, Mary is heard laughing. It's a melodic giggle, without any of the sharp precision of her speaking voice.

"All right, I'm just getting started." Charlie picks himself up and hacks away at the wall. The first few hits only shake more plaster free, and expose a larger area of thin, wooden slats. Then, with a grunt of exertion, he punches through the wall down near the baseboard, burying the hammer's head in it.

Charlie leverages the solid metal end against the wood and pries out two of the boards, opening a gap. He keeps at it and soon has a hole about three or four feet wide that stops just below his knees. Nothing but darkness can be seen inside the void.

"Whoa. Whoa. What's that?" Mary takes the camera off the tripod and everything gets much brighter as the light comes on. The glare forces Charlie to shade his eyes as she heads toward him.

"What are you doing?" he asks.

Mary doesn't answer. She passes Charlie and leans down. The light shines inside the dusty cavity.

"The space between the walls," she says. "It goes back too far."

"Let me see." Charlie nudges her aside and peers in. "It's like there's a whole other room in there."

He gets up and walks off-screen. When he comes back, he has a long yellow crowbar. "Like I always say, use the right tool for the job." Charlie pulls more slats away with brute force lunges until the gap is large enough for him to crawl through.

Kneeling in the dark space, he reaches out and asks for the camera.

Everything blurs in the fast pan of the video recorder switching from one set of hands to another. When it steadies again, the scene is of a claustrophobic nook entirely clad in narrow slats. The wood has darkened with age to a deep mahogany shade. It's empty except for the motes of dust caught in the light's beam. It isn't really a room as Charlie suggested. It's only wide enough to cram his body into — his knees are pressed together, clamped by the walls — and the passage ends mere feet from the lens.

Charlie shifts around in the tight space to see what's in the other direction. Still crouching, his movements are jerky and hesitant. The first time watching the footage, the anticipation is so strong it makes his slowness painful to sit through. Why doesn't he just angle the camera over his shoulder? Or stand up so he could maneuver easier?

On the second viewing, there's dread. It's easy to hope he won't turn around. To wish he'd get out of there and never find what this hidden room contains. Perhaps if he never turns around, it won't be there. Maybe, like some quantum particle, it only exists once it's observed.

When the camera has made a full one-eighty, it focuses on a corridor stretching into the distance. Perhaps it's the angles that make it seem as though the space extends farther than it has any right to. Or it might be a trick of the lens and it wouldn't look so terrifyingly long to the naked eye. But probably not, because Charlie's breath has grown short and raspy and a subtle tremor runs through the hand holding the camera.

Mary calls to him. "What is it?"

"There's something in here." He stands, shimmying himself up the wall. With the elevation, it begins to feel more like a mine shaft than a crawlspace.

The light focuses on an abstract heap against the far wall. Charlie heads toward it. With each slow, cautious step, the object takes on the shape of a table. The top is gray with an irregular surface resembling a model of a desert plain, dotted with mesas. A black drape hangs from it and pools on the floor.

A little closer and the gray hills crystalize into candles, burnt and melted until all the wax has congealed to form a single slab. Dozens of pillar and taper candles have transformed into a swirling mass of whites, blacks, and reds, with only a few towers and domes remaining to identify what they once were.

The camera tilts up and gets a good look at the wall behind it. A symbol is scrawled in chalk on the dark, almost black, wood. But is it chalk? After all the years it must have been here, how could chalk still look this fresh and white? So white, it glows in the light. The symbol itself is reminiscent of a capital G. It's drawn with a sweeping half-circle and has a fishhook forming the tail.

"Daddy, what did you find?" A child's voice echoes in the secret hallway, making it sound uncannily real, as though the little boy was standing right on the other side of the computer screen.

"Richie, get back. Don't come in here. Mary, keep him out of here."

"What is it?" Unlike the boy's voice, Mary's sounds weak and distant, closer to a memory than real words.

Charlie reaches the altar. There's a glint in the swirling tidal pool of wax. A knife is half buried in the mess. It's a long, thin dagger and the blade is stained dark with rust.

Or does it only look like rust? Why isn't more than just the edge oxidized? Why hasn't it spread to the rest of the steel?

Perhaps Charlie is thinking the same thing as his hand reaches down, almost unconsciously, to test its surface.

"It's nothing," he yells back to his family, right before the footage ends. Right before he touches the blade.

2.

THE YELLOWS AND REDS OF A DEAD LEAF lying by the toe of Molly's boot spoke of summer's end. An overnight rain had plastered it to the pavement, and even after drying in the morning sun, the wind couldn't move it. It stayed glued in place like a fly in a web, waiting to rot or be worn away piece by piece by the people who passed through the park on their way to somewhere else.

"Earth to Molly," Kevin said.

Startled by his presence, she looked up and stood in one swift motion, locking him in an embrace. "Thanks for meeting me."

"How could I turn down a free lunch?" The wide smile that told her he was joking shrank to a more natural, concerned expression. "So, what gives?"

They sat down next to each other on the park bench.

"I needed to get some air." She rummaged in her backpack and took out two sandwiches.

"Frustrating morning?"

"You have no idea." She held them out, one in each hand. "Turkey or egg?"

"Well, they say you are what you eat. I'll have the turkey." His mouth flashed the same self-conscious smile as before, but Molly was unable to manage her usual grin. The faint headache behind her eyes only emphasized how many times she'd heard the joke before.

"You still haven't found anything?"

"Nothing. It's like the Internet has been scrubbed." The video had shown the web address of the couple's blog, but that only generated a *404 page not found* error. She knew their names, but neither search engines nor a stalker-like perusal of social media had turned up anything.

The Garrisons' discovery had been posted on a site called *The Haunted Web*. The written comments were a bit more detailed than what Keith had told her at dinner but it was short on specifics and facts. It said that after the scene was filmed, the Garrisons experienced a series of accidents involving multiple trips to the hospital, becoming more severe until one of the sons vanished. It didn't mention which of the boys it was or what had happened to the rest of the family.

Molly contacted the writer and began tracing back a series of re-postings from sites and blogs until reaching a webpage in Japan, run by a teenager who didn't speak a word of English. From there, the trail went cold.

The symbol drawn on the wall was easier to track down. There was even a handy animation explaining it on a website that catalogued a host of demons. It turned out to be the sigil for some nasty-looking thing called Hismael. But the reason why anyone would set up an altar to it in their home was missing from both the video and all the literature she could find on Hismael or demon worship in general.

And the purpose of sealing the altar behind a wall was an even greater mystery.

Half of Kevin's sandwich had disappeared before he spoke again. "I don't understand why you can't use what you have. It sounds like a story to me."

"Yeah, what I have would be wonderful if I was writing some throwaway article for a blog that didn't care about facts, but this is my thesis. I need to find a real-life event that becomes twisted into a strange, fictitious story. And right now, I can't prove this tape is real. Where did it take place? Who are these people? Where did they go?"

"Calm down. I'm only trying to help."

"I know. It's just…" The bitter onion in the egg salad lingered on Molly's tongue. Market Square's lunch crowd buzzed around them. The benches were full and a few people sat on the grass, but most crossed back and forth, using it as a shortcut to reach the stores and restaurants surrounding the park.

Kevin didn't understand why this was important to her. To him, life was about checking the boxes. Go to school: check. Get a job: check. Get married: check. Have kids: check—check—check. She loved him, but they were such different people. To her, this wasn't about getting her master's and going onto the next step, it was about making an impact in her field. She needed to show her professors and peers Molly Heyworth was more than someone passing through. She was special. She had a killer theory about how these urban legends grew in the Internet age, but she needed to prove it.

"I'm sorry if I said something wrong." Kevin wrapped his arm around her shoulders. The weight of it provided the same comfort as a snug blanket and she turned to nestle into his chest. The wool of his suit was rough against her cheek but she didn't pull away.

"No, you're right. I should toss it in the pile with my other rejected topics and move on."

Kevin rocked her gently. "I didn't say that. If it means so much to you, you should keep at it. It's the Internet. Nothing disappears. Post a stupid picture of yourself at a college party and it will be there, somewhere, waiting to embarrass you when you're sixty years old."

"I'll give it another shot," she said, tilting her face toward his. "But I'm not getting my hopes up. I can't waste the rest of my life on this. If nothing turns up in a couple of days...*sayonara.*" Molly ran her finger across her throat.

HISMAEL: THE ACQUIRER

THE PICTURE IS ANNOYINGLY SMALL. It's not even the size of a smartphone screen and it's almost lost on the burgundy webpage crowded with blocks of gold text and numerous faint, arcane symbols showing through like digital watermarks. The video's window can't be enlarged or resized and a hyperkinetic ad for toothpaste plays on a loop below it adding to the distraction.

The static image of the G-shaped sigil against a sepia background fills the frame. Three seconds in, it's unclear if the video is even working, but then the symbol begins falling backward and diminishing until it forms only a small dot in the distance. It's replaced by an elaborately sketched roman numeral and the title is read in a raspy voiceover: "Number eight, Hismael, The Acquirer."

The words in the tiny window dissolve and a hulking, hunched figure enters. Drawn in the style of an old woodcut, the creature is all spidery black lines suggesting shapes and crevices with crosshatched shadows. The ink has life. The lines shift, fade, and reform as the creature moves into view, revealing a chimera monster with a furry body, elephant-like legs, and a snapping serpent for a tail.

It's comical, cute even. It could be an escapee from *Where the Wild Things Are*, except as talented as the animator is, he's a far cry from Maurice Sendak.

The creature shuffles into the center and turns its horned head to the viewer. Sadness haunts its bovine eyes.

"One of the original angels to rebel with Lucifer," the voice continues. The speaker is trying to both project for the microphone and talk in an eerie hush. The effect is juvenile and invokes an image of a teenager doing the narration in a dark basement.

"He was cast down to Hell, where he served his new master by going out into the world and obtaining objects of power and souls of great worth. After a failed quest, his wings were torn off and he went mad, descending into the lost pits of the underworld to nurse his wounds and grow his despair."

Even though the creature is standing still, its eyes still move as though searching something out beyond the screen.

"Hismael is linked to Jupiter and if you plan on summoning him, you must ensure that the planet is in the night sky. But beware, he is unpredictable and uncontrollable. If you are not careful, you might be the next soul he acquires."

3.

KEVIN CAME IN from his morning jog, panting from the run and from climbing the four flights of stairs to their apartment. Keys hit the glass tray by the door, followed by the *whump* of a sneaker being kicked off and then another.

The animal smell of his sweat met Molly a moment before his hand gripped the back of her chair.

"So, how goes it? Struck any gold?"

"This is amazing," she said, not taking her eyes off her notebook, where the blank whiteness was rapidly being replaced by the tight loops and sharp strokes of blue ink, describing the last video she'd watched.

Molly had spent the rest of the week trying to find more information about the Garrisons with no better luck than she had at the beginning. She'd all but given up when there was a response to a post she'd left on an Internet forum. The guy — or possibly girl — named Tailspin747 had watched most of the original *Garrison Project* when it was online two years ago. And through some amazing luck, Tailspin747 was tech savvy enough to pull the old files from his hard drive.

Molly had woken up that Saturday morning to find the first eight installments in her inbox.

"Did they capture any ghosts on film?" Kevin asked.

She shook her head. "Don't be silly." Molly was in too good a mood to get drawn into his teasing. Ghosts didn't interest her in the least. What she was after was a regular family caught in an urban myth because of people's morbid speculation. And so far, the tapes were perfect — everything was perfectly ordinary.

The first episode was a walkthrough of the unrenovated property with Mary and Charlie discussing what they hated and what they were planning on doing.

It was a poky two-story cottage. The white paint on its exterior was flaking off and the black specks it left behind resembled spores of mold spreading across the front. Except for having another house pressed in close on one side, it appeared to be in the middle of the woods. Dozens of maples and pines cast permanent shade upon the home and yard. Charlie explained how it was built as a summer cottage but had been winterized in the sixties, when the tiny mountain community was incorporated into the sprawling suburbs.

Everything in the house was old, outdated, and worn. There didn't seem to be a single thing the couple didn't plan to rip out or change.

The next installment was the one with the strange altar. Molly hoped there might be more to this version, but it still ended abruptly with Charlie Garrison about to touch the knife.

After that, the episodes only showed normal home renovations: laying new floors, installing a bathtub, building kitchen cabinets. There were some accidents but nothing out of the ordinary. In fact, if something seemed strange to Molly, it was the complete absence of any mention of that spooky altar. In the fourth installment, they revealed the finished dining room, now running the entire length of the home. It was a seamless room with a bright coat of pale, yellow paint. There was no sign that the hidden hall or the sigil had ever been there and nothing was said to remind anyone about it.

"So, no ghosts?" Kevin's persistence was growing irritating. But there was something endearing about it as well. The way he was trying to capture her full attention hinted at the little boy he once was — still was, sometimes.

"The scariest things they've come across were some dead mice and a nest of carpenter ants." Molly finished up the last of her notes and twisted in her chair to speak to him. His face was still red and shining from his run. His damp shirt clung to the muscles of his arms and chest. For an accountant, he was still as buff as the track star she'd first started dating.

"Sounds boring. I was hoping there would be ghouls creeping through the house while the family slept. Or they'd find human sacrifices in the root cellar."

"Ugh, gross."

"I like gross."

"Then you should watch episode five. They replace a crumbling plumbing stack." Molly made an exaggerated shudder as though the memory might induce vomiting.

"All done then?"

"I just have one more to watch."

"You know, you left bed awfully early this morning." Kevin leaned into her. "Why don't you put this aside for a while? I think you forgot something in there." His heated hand ran up her arm. "Perhaps I can help you find it."

Molly pushed him back. "You stink. Go take a shower." She let her scowl turn into a smile, drawing it out for effect. "I'll come when you're not so...gross."

DAY 36: ARTS AND CRAFTS

MARY STANDS in the middle of the living room. The ponytail tying back her hair makes her forehead look high and her skin tight. The plaid shirt she wears is boyish but the white tank top underneath has a low V-neck showing a hint of cleavage. A paintbrush is in her hand. It's much more delicate than the utility brushes they used to paint the walls.

"Today we're taking a little break from the hard work to do an art project for our fabulous new kitchen. I'm going to be making a sign that recalls an old-time farmer's market. And I'll show you how you can do it too."

"Hold up the inspiration." From the sound of Charlie's voice, he must be giving instruction from behind the camera.

"Oh right." Mary digs around on the makeshift work-bench constructed from two sawhorses and an old door. She lifts a cut-out from a magazine. "I came across this…"

The five-year-old comes into the room from the foyer. He's on his hands and knees pushing a toy car. The wheels make a horrible squeaking sound against the floor reminiscent of nails on a blackboard.

The boy's blond hair is like his father's, only brighter, as if Charlie's had tarnished over the years. He's barefoot and his red T-shirt has a graphic of a black dog on the front.

"Richie, stay out of here. Mommy and Daddy are working."

The boy ignores his mother and continues to push the toy through the shot and into the kitchen. Mary tries to speak over the screeching of the plastic tires, explaining how she came across the picture in an antiques magazine. She tries to give the reasons why the concept will fit in perfectly with their country-chic kitchen, but the noise is too much of a distraction and she says, "Um," every few words.

When Richie is gone and the sound has faded, she holds up a wooden panel in the shape of a heraldic shield. "This fine piece of craftsmanship is courtesy of my handy hubby."

Off-screen, Charlie says, "Thank you, thank you," as though he's taking a bow to applause.

"As you can see, he used two pieces of oak and cut the pattern out with a jigsaw. It's been stained and distressed to give it a sense of age. Now I'm going to paint the design on it. First, I'll start with the white paint and then layer on the other colors. I just need to get this open."

While Mary's struggling with the jar, Henry dashes into the room, jerking to a stop at the workbench. He's the older son and must be about nine or so. His thin body is dressed for summer in shorts and a T-shirt but his right arm is in a sling. He also has a cut along the left side of his forehead, only partially hidden by his shaggy brown hair.

"Mom, Mom! Can I have a popsicle?"

"Can't you see I'm busy?" Mary says. The lid is yanked off and a stream of milky white paint spills down her wrist.

"Dad. Can I have a popsicle?"

"Sure. But only one."

Richie comes around the corner again. Without the wall in the dining room, the entire downstairs makes a loop the boy can follow like a racetrack circuit. The squeal takes over the room again, and with the sharp increase in the pitch of the noise, there is the realization that it never stopped. It has always been lurking in the background, muffled and dissipated by distance and walls. It's accompanied by the shuffling and knocking of his denim-clad legs and the slapping of his hand on the new hardwood floors.

"Both you boys get on out of here." Charlie waves a bruised and bandaged hand at them, and the camera catches the ugliness of the healing process in an out-of-focus close-up.

When Mary has the stage to herself again, she begins to paint the lettering at the top of the board freehand. Charlie carries the camera over to film her work. With smooth strokes, she writes the words *Farmers* and *Market* as they appeared in the clipping: one above the other and the F and S of *Farmers* oversized to bracket both words.

The first time the tape is watched, it is easy to be caught up with her skill and steady hand. But the second time around, the background sounds become agonizingly clear.

Mary is humming as she works and Charlie makes no noise.

Henry is in the kitchen. The freezer door opens and closes. A wrapper is torn. A chair drags across the tile floor with a brief scrape.

Then there's the noise of Richie and his car. The constant squeak-squeak of the toy and the thump-thump of his knees dwindle as he moves farther away from the camera. But it's still there. It takes an attentive ear, but he can be heard crossing through the dining room.

Then right around the point on the tape when the K in *Market* is being drawn and when Henry is pulling the chair, there's an absence.

Beyond Mary's humming, the little plastic wheels still let out their shrill whine, but the banging of Richie's hands and knees is gone.

The high-pitched squeal of the toy rises in volume and Charlie swings the camera over to the doorway. "I thought I told you–"

The little replica of a police squad car comes rolling into the room and hits the wall. Now, there is nothing but absolute silence in the house.

"Richie?" The nervous strain Charlie uses to say his son's name makes it easy to speculate he already knows something is wrong. "Come pick up your things. Richie?"

Maybe they both know, because Mary drops the brush. It tumbles to the ground and leaves a paint smear on the floor but Mary doesn't notice. She's already rushing out through the entryway, limping and calling for her little boy. The camera stays focused on the empty doorway. From far away, she says, "Henry, where's your brother?"

4.

THE CHURCH BELLS from St. Michael's rang out at the end of mass. From her window, Molly could see the steeple poking above the rooftops, with the clear, autumn sunlight glinting off its cross.

Kevin sat at the kitchen table behind her reading the Sunday paper. The way he crinkled the pages every few minutes had taken on the quality of fingers drumming with impatience. It was either Molly's imagination or a rare display of passive aggressive behavior.

Molly put her earphones on, dreaming about how nice it would be to have an office with some privacy. Maybe one day, when her career was important enough, she'd have her own room to work in peace. She pushed play and the video came on with the title card, *Day 19: A Horrible Surprise.*

How many times has she watched them rip out the old moldy plaster to discover the crumbling plumbing stack? It must've been at least the fourth. However many viewings, it was enough to desensitize her to the revolting shots of the sewage-slimed shaft leading down to the basement.

Even though the title said the events of the episode took place on day nineteen, it was clearly filmed over more than one day, since by the time they were ready to put the new stack in, night had become day and they were wearing a third set of clothes (their original outfits having been ruined by the discovery). Most of the footage had been severely edited, reducing the hours spent pumping out the old pipe and the many trips to the hardware store to a handful of minutes of screen time, making it impossible to know how long a period was actually being presented.

The episode was nearing its end when Kevin hugged Molly from behind and kissed her neck. He hadn't made a sound coming over and her muscles tensed at the unexpectedness of his touch. She sat rigid in his arms, only relaxing into the embrace once it was already slackening and evaporating into nothing but a hand on her shoulder.

Kevin mimed taking off the headphones. Molly pressed pause and pulled the buds from her ears.

"It's a beautiful day out there. Why don't we run by the market and pick up stuff for a picnic? We can go down to Castell Park and sit by the water."

"You can grab lunch without me. Head down to the Bee and the Bonnet, if you want. I have a lot of work to do." It would be a relief to have the apartment to herself.

"You don't want to work too hard on Sunday, it's bad luck."

"I think you mean, sacrilegious. Too bad, I'm not Catholic, Mr. O'Brien." She gave him a quick peck on the cheek. "Have a beer for me. Got to get back to it."

Molly picked up her earbuds but Kevin took her hand, stopping her from going back to the Garrisons. "You've been watching those things for two days straight."

That was a gross exaggeration. Molly hadn't even had the videos for two full days. She dropped the wires and faced him. "Can't you understand? This is a major discovery. I need to go over these."

"What are you going to find in those videos you haven't already seen?"

Molly's words stalled. How could she explain it to him? The first viewing had been enough to show her how the urban legend had begun: the demonic altar, all the accidents, the missing boy. But with each progressive re-watching, the subtle drama of the family unfolded, like stripping away the layers of wallpaper in an antique house. The strain on their marriage, their money problems, Charlie's moments of rage. These elements began to bleed through the quaint home improvement episodes. Molly was beginning to see beyond the fogged filter the tapes created and get a better understanding of the Garrisons. She was close to a breakthrough. If only she'd be left alone.

"Hey. Hey. Don't get upset," Kevin said, somehow reading her mood from whatever subtle twitch of her lips or brow had betrayed her thoughts. His face softened and he knelt by the desk clasping her hands. "All I'm saying is this might be the last nice weekend we have. November is around the corner. I want to go out and enjoy this beautiful weather with my beautiful wife. Come on. It'll be fun. And this will all be waiting for you when you get back."

He was right. It would soon be winter. First the cold, gray rains would come and rip any remaining leaves from the trees. Then the snow would bury the town in a pristine white blanket. It would be perfect for Christmas but would grow dingier and less welcome as time dragged on. It would be months until spring and another day when they could go for a picnic.

"All right," she said. "Let me finish this episode and we'll go. Five minutes."

Kevin gave her a smile that was part genuine happiness but mostly showed his relief. "Five minutes," he repeated. "I'll hold you to it."

He sat on the couch and pulled up a game on his phone to kill time while he waited.

Molly pressed play. There wasn't much more in the installment. Mary poured a bucket of water down the new pipe and declared it a success. Charlie kissed her and they waved goodbye to the viewers in one of their typical hokey endings.

The mouse cursor hovered over the next file. Molly glanced over her shoulder. Kevin was still absorbed in his game, his thumbs flicking across the screen. She had time for one more.

DAY 22: A NEW BATHROOM

AFTER THE TITLE FADES OFF the screen, Mary is in the bathroom doorway. The way the camera is angled upward suggests Charlie is standing on the stairs to keep her at a medium focal distance.

"This is Mary Garrison." There's an emptiness to the scene with her standing all by herself. The awkward, small flexing of her arms and knees amplifies her isolation. "Today we will be finishing the bathroom. In a house with two boys, it can't come fast enough." She leans a hand on the door sill. The pose is almost seductive, except it's obvious nothing sexual is going through her head as she looks at the lens and Charlie. Her eyes are too tired. They're rimmed with red and the lids droop. She's smiling but her lips are thin and severe.

"Now that the waste stack has been repaired — finally — and the plumbing is all fixed and ready to go, we only need to get the new fixtures installed." She backs up into the room and switches on the light. The camera follows making jerky movements as Charlie climbs up to the landing.

"We've decided to salvage the original floor." She makes a downward gesture and the view tilts filling the screen with black and white hexagonal tiles. At first glance, it is easy to see their vintage appeal but while Mary explains the choice, the camera lingers on them and the numerous cracks and chips become apparent. "It wasn't our original plan. Instead of ripping the floor up, we've been over it with a brush and vinegar. And that worked, somewhat. It put a shine on them. Still not the same as new, but we have to cut costs where we can." Something bitter is carried on her words and despite their surface meaning, she's obviously not in agreement with the decision.

The position of the camera waivers and sinks toward the floor with neglect. Charlie says her name. It's used as both a warning and a full stop, a pre-emptive strike closing the debate. It doesn't take much imagination for their whole argument to be conjured up by that one word.

"I know." Her face is still off-camera and the acoustics of the room distort her voice, making it impossible to determine with any certainty what she means by it. Does she know the reason why they have to leave these old broken tiles and she's sorry she brought it up? Does she know she shouldn't be returning to this disagreement on-camera? Does she know where things will lead if she continues to express her own opinion?

Perhaps this last possibility hits closest to the truth because when the lens is lifted to her again, Mary is facing away with her hand by her eyes as though she's wiping away a sadness before it can fully seize her.

"So." Here she gives an over-the-shoulder glance at her audience, her lips in a strained smile. "We're also keeping the same layout. Anything different would involve taking space from one of the bedrooms, and that would mean moving walls, and...well, we're not prepared to do that."

In the re-watching, it is tempting to think this might to be a hint at some other fight. After all, they were prepared to tear down walls downstairs, so why not up here? Has this whole project been a series of losing battles for Mary?

She faces the camera full-on and her next words, with their relaxed tone, dispel those thoughts. "The bedrooms have no space to spare. And as nice as it might be to put in a double sink or a separate shower, it's functional enough for us." Said differently it would come across as complaining but Mary approaches the limitations with a return to her usual on-air chipperness, making lemonade out of what life has given her. Her smile is no longer forced and she doesn't fidget as she goes around explaining the work they'll be doing.

Despite Mary's lighter mood, the tension is maintained by the way the sequence is shot. In the tight space, she always appears to be pressed up against the wall, moving from corner to corner, while Charlie silently stalks her with the camera. The only times he speaks is to prompt her with details she has forgotten or hasn't gotten to fast enough.

Having gone through the tapes so many times, it has become a Mobius strip of ever-looping events, without beginning or end. And the clawing emotional distress between them makes it easy to forget this episode takes place two full weeks before their son's disappearance.

Once they're finished with the introductory spiel, there's a cut and the next image is of the new claw-foot tub occupying the previously empty void. Charlie is lying on the floor next to it, reaching for the shut-off valve in the tight gap between the wall and tub. The camera is set on a tripod giving a voyeuristic angle through the open doorway. Mary has switched it on and for a moment the view is obscured by her body as she crosses through the frame to enter the room.

She's visible only for the second or two it takes her to slip inside and go to the corner beside the door. Charlie gets his fingers on the lever and turns the water back on, saying, "There." He sits up to try the faucet. After a gasping sputter, the water first sprays, then pours into the tub. Shutting the tap off, he gives a satisfied look to the lens before getting up.

Mary's movement from camera to corner gets lost in the early viewings. Initially, the focus is directed on Charlie and Mary is ignored. Then, once the ending is known, it's hard to pay attention to this business with the bathtub. It's nothing but an irrelevant digression while impatiently waiting for Mary's accident. The fall she will take down the stairs in a few minutes casts a long shadow. It's an incident that weighs as heavily on the present as it does on the future — a future that has already happened over and over again on the computer screen. It is only through the numbing of the shock and the erosion of time itself that Mary's few simple steps gain meaning.

Mary's first step: A quarter of the screen is taken up by her hip and the faded denim of her jeans, made black by the lack of light.

Steps two and three: Mary's bottom eclipses all but a sliver on the left of the screen.

Step four: The sound changes. The barely-there noise of sneaker on wood is replaced by the tap of hard rubber on the tiling. Her body takes on regular proportions and the bathroom is seen beside her.

Step five: Another tap and Mary's profile and shoulder appear in the medicine cabinet mirror.

Steps six and seven: *Tap, tap.* Her head appears in the mirror, followed by her ponytail. The cross-purpose angles of the camera and the mirror are disorienting. They make it appear as though a double is entering from another door, a doppelgänger on its way to meet Mary in the center of the room. But Mary goes to the right instead.

Step eight: The real Mary is seen from the side before passing out of sight. The other Mary walks away from the camera.

Step nine: Mary's reflection leaves the camera frame as well.

Tap. Tap. Tap. She keeps walking.

But where does she go?

The mirror shows the empty corner. The wall beside it is in the shot and if she was moving farther into the room, she'd be visible. If she was to continue going to the right, Molly would enter Richie's bedroom, except a wall is blocking her.

The most rational explanation is the sound is caused by her pivoting in place, while in a blind spot created by the angle of the lens and the mirror. But it's hard to shake the eerie feeling that she has slipped out of reality.

When Mary leaves her hiding spot, Charlie is talking and making too much noise for the viewer to count her steps and prove that she was in the corner the whole time. So doubt lingers.

"Okay," he says. "Now for the vanity. Everything is going like clockwork. We should have a fully functioning bathroom by dinner time."

Mary follows him into the hall where the new sink is stashed. They squabble over the best way to hold it when lifting and grunt with exertion. Nothing is on-camera except the vacant bathroom. Their labors exist only in the mind of the viewer. Then there is a thud. The camera rocks in its mount and Charlie shouts, "Damn it! I told you not to let it slip."

Mary mutters an incoherent apology. What happens next is also left to the imagination. Presumably, Mary stumbles backward and trips. A brief flash of her white shirt is captured in the corner of the frame, then her ponytail fans out a spray of dark hair in front of the lens. She is tumbling across the landing. Each of the thumps that follow invokes a cringe as her body bounces down the stairs.

"Mary. Mary!" Charlie is calling. The urgent strain in his voice suggests he's fearing the worst.

"I'm okay," she says. The words are so far away, they're no louder than a hiss on the mic. Charlie begins to head downstairs. "No. Stay where you are. It's just my ankle. I'll be all right."

Charlie hesitates, watching his injured wife from above. Instead of going to her, he backs up and turns off the camera.

5.

MOLLY'S HUNCHED OVER THE PAGE, her arms encircling it as though her body was an army laying siege to a fortress. Her concentration was total as she marked down each path with care. The felt pen glided along in the wake of the Garrisons' footsteps, while the rest of the world fell away like a half-remembered dream.

"Didn't you go to school today? Are you sick?" Kevin said.

Molly jerked upright with a heart-thumping burst of adrenaline. He was home. For how long?

The desk lamp projected her ghostly image on the window. When had night fallen? Autumn brought shorter days, but the last time she looked out, the copper roof on the building across the street had been shining in the sun.

Her reflection showed a woman with wan, drawn skin. The hair rising from her scalp resembled wild grass in the wind. She ran a hand through it, but it was a poor replacement for shampoo and a brush. When the worst strands were patted down, Molly pushed her glasses back from the tip of her nose.

She frowned at the pajama pants and camisole she'd been wearing since last night. *Please don't ask me why I'm not dressed yet,* she willed, getting up to kiss Kevin hello. "No, not sick."

To draw questions away from herself, Molly asked him about his day and feigned interest as she got him to share the mundane details of work and office politics. All the while, the Garrisons and their every step trudged through her mind, as though the floorplan of that accursed house was imprinted there.

When Kevin had finished his stories and grumbles, when his jacket was off and his tie slung across the back of the sofa, he approached her and took each of her arms in his hands. "What's up with you?"

The question was one he may have asked a thousand times before, but his tone brimmed with concern. His unwanted pity left Molly with a sickening feeling, as though he had called her an imbecile or a child. She pulled away, trying to avoid the implications and latch onto the base meaning of the question. To lose herself in the insult would be to fall into a pit. Its slippery walls were already pulling her down into the depths of darkness. It was better to wipe the tear from her eye before it came and ignore it.

"Kevin, you'll never believe what I found." Molly went to the desk and picked up her work. The leather folio in her hands brought back all the excitement she'd been feeling and rekindled her enthusiasm. She forgot the look in Kevin's eyes as well as her deep wish that he'd go back out and leave her alone. Molly adjusted the graph paper and the clear acetate sheets to show off her discovery. A nervous tingling of exhaustion and euphoria began in her fingertips and spread through her whole body.

"While I was re-watching the episodes this morning, I noticed something strange in the sixth one — you know, when they're working on the bathroom. And then something even stranger after the accident in the kitchen. So I started plotting out the family's movements, using a different color for each person. Red for Mary, blue for Charlie, green for— well, you get the picture. That doesn't really matter. What matters is this: look." She handed him the leather folder displaying the page labeled, "Day 29, ground floor."

On the translucent plastic, an odd series of swirls with branching tangents mapped the paths of each of the family members. Most of the activity was centered on the kitchen, with mad scribbles of blue and red snaking around one another.

"I have no idea what I'm looking at," Kevin said.

"Watch the dining room. I happened to notice it after Charlie hurts his hand. I had to guess a bit at his exact steps, because while he's running for the first aid kit, the footage is a mess." Molly followed the blue line out of the kitchen with her finger to demonstrate. "But then, while Mary is talking to him, he turns — he turns, Kevin." She nearly screams this. Her voice is uncharacteristically high to her own ears. She's staring at the page so closely she needs to brush her hair off so he can see it.

"I still don't get it."

"He turns. So when he starts walking again, he should head straight into the wall. But somehow, he goes through to the foyer instead." Molly said *foyer* precisely how Mary had coached. "Look. See. He never turns back again. Technically, Charlie walks through the wall. If you follow his exact steps as he takes them, they spiral into the center of the house. I don't know how, but the house moves around him, otherwise he'd end up down the basement stairs instead up in the bathroom."

"That doesn't make any sense." Kevin studied it, taking the folio away from her and bringing it up to his face.

"I know. Something supernatural is at work."

"I thought you said there wasn't anything supernatural about those tapes."

"Well, that was before I found this. It's incredible."

Kevin gave her a skeptical look and sighed. "This is insane."

The pit opened at her feet again, the darkness lapped at her ankles. Must he dismiss everything she did? Just because it wasn't as straight and orderly as the columns of numbers in his ledgers didn't make her work crazy.

His back faced Molly and he couldn't see her glaring at him or the anger coloring her cheeks. He flipped through the pages spending a few seconds studying each one. Molly wanted to rip the folio from his hands. He shouldn't be touching her hard work.

The folder contained two sheets of graph paper with layouts for both floors in the Garrisons' house. Molly had drawn them with the exactness of a blueprint. For each floor, there were eight plastic overlays representing an episode.

Kevin's study shortened the deeper into the book he got and soon he was turning the sheets over with only a cursory glance. "Molly, you need to take a break from this. You're losing it. You need a good night's sleep. This isn't healthy. I really think..."

He got to the last sheet and stopped. He'd been walking across the room, pacing in his distraction, when he froze mid-stride, his eyes riveted on the page and his mouth working, as though literally chewing on his thoughts.

"I didn't expect you to understand. I have uncovered something amazing. Something special. Something that will make me—"

"Molly, tell me you did this on purpose?" A tremor softened his voice and his face had paled a degree.

Kevin's fear was contagious and Molly felt a chill spreading through the room. Because the horror at the bottom of the pit was the very frightening and very distinct possibility that her interest in the tapes might no longer be sane. Did Kevin have in his hands proof that Molly had done something crazy?

"What?" The word was spoken with only her lips, no sound escaped.

"Tell me this is a joke. Say you're putting me on. Say 'gotcha' and laugh at me. Get it over with."

"What are you talking about?"

He turned the folio for her to see.

With all the acetates piled on top of each other, there was a confusion of overlapping paths. The eight Garrison feet had traced almost every square inch of the home. But a pattern emerged. Like the scrawl of an obsessed mind running a pen over the same figure again and again, until the separate colors of the family members became black in their merging and formed a symbol. The other paths looked feeble around it, mere threads stretching out from a great horrific web. When viewed together, the Garrisons' steps filled the house with Hismael's sigil exactly as it had been drawn over the altar.

DAY 29: KITCHEN TRANSFORMATION

CHARLIE IS CUTTING the support beams for the kitchen island. The camera clipped onto his work vest captures his hands as he runs the circular saw through the lumber. A fine spray of sawdust fills the air.

It's only after he's done and the blade spins to a groaning stop that Mary can be heard saying, "—designed by the Devil."

"What?"

"Satan made this stupid faucet. There's no way to get a hold of these bolts."

The camera pans to the sink. Mary is on her back and her bare legs stick out of the newly installed cabinet. From how it's mounted, the camera aims down at an angle and makes it appear that Charlie is staring at her smooth, tanned thighs. Mary bends her left leg and the compression bandage around her ankle comes into frame.

"Do you want me to do that?" Charlie asks.

"No, I got it. If only there was more room to work under here."

A metallic click rings out from under the sink and Mary curses. "The wrench keeps slipping."

Charlie keeps watching. The sink they've put in is a large porcelain farmhouse style. It looks antique but isn't. The faucet is tall and industrial, bought at auction from a restaurant bankruptcy. The high spout wobbles in place as Mary works on it from underneath.

"Well, don't just stand there," she yells to him from her lair. "We're on a schedule."

"Yes, ma'am," he says in a mock Southern drawl and trudges off to the site of the kitchen island. Even though it takes longer, he circles around the workbench, as though compelled to take a wider path across the floor. When he gets to the half-built frame, he picks up one of the cut two-by-fours and his pneumatic hammer.

"We want the nails to go in cleanly so I'm going with this fellow. Remember, always use the right tool for the job." He clicks on the trigger a couple of times cowboy style. Without the tip depressed against the wood, the gun only makes harmless clicks. He sticks the board on the wall and holds it in place with his left hand.

"Now, this won't be too pretty at first," he tells the viewer. "It's only the frame I'm building, but once we cover the posts in reclaimed barn-board, it's going to look amazing."

With each nail, the compressor lets out a sharp spitting sound. *Ptew.* He puts a nail in every two inches working his way up toward his hand. *Ptew. Ptew.*

Charlie places the nail-gun right in the space between his thumb and index finger readying the last fastener.

"Ugh, I'm sweating like a pig." Mary's words comes over the mic with alarming volume. Charlie jumps and the camera jerks.

Ptew.

Charlie's voice is strident with rage as he stands and faces her. "What the hell? Don't sneak up on me like that."

"Are you all right?"

"Yeah, fine. You just surprised me."

"Sorry. But I'm all done. Do you want to give the faucet a try?"

"Later." His tone is softer but his hostility remains. With each progressive viewing, Charlie's temper seems more pronounced. His small outbursts of fury become amplified until it is hard to remember the moments when he's not angry.

He speaks with forced patience, drawing each word out as a separate sentence. "Let me get this done, okay?"

"O-kay." No matter how many times the tape is played, it is impossible to tell if Mary is mocking him or if she's mimicking his tone in one of those intimate quirks of language lovers share and which are ingrained into a relationship the way lines are inked into a script.

By the hundredth viewing or so, a braveness can be felt. As the camera leers at her chest and cuts off the top of her head, it doesn't matter if Mary's *okay* is meant as a challenge or to placate him. Either way, she's standing against this big, brutish man — this man whose movie-star looks are nothing but wool hiding the wolf. A sense he may hit her for not demurring to him lingers. But Mary stands unflinching.

If violence is lurking in Charlie's mind, it will never be known, because they are interrupted by Richie wandering into the work site.

The blond-haired tot walks with uneven steps. Left slow. Right fast. As though walking itself is a game.

"Mom-my." He speaks in singsong, matching the odd rhythm of his steps.

Mary and Charlie speak at the same time.

"What is it?" she says.

"I told you to stay out of here. Why don't you ever listen?" Charlie advances on the boy.

Richie backs away, bumping into one of the discarded pieces of scaffolding leaning against the wall. The boy is so small and the nudge so slight that it shouldn't be able to move the heavy, metal framework. It must've been placed there precariously. It's the only rational way to explain how it immediately begins to shift when it's touched.

It teeters, dropping toward the camera, gaining momentum as the balance tips. Charlie races for his boy and pushes him out of the way.

This is the last clear image in the kitchen before frenetic motion takes over, distorting the next several seconds.

There's a clang. A scream. A string of profanity. The camera goes wild with Charlie's thrashing. It bounces and spins. Then he makes a wobbly, seasickness-inducing run, accompanied by an incomprehensible incantation, where the phrase, "My hand. My hand," repeats interspersed with a machinegun discharge of *fucks, shits,* and *goddamn-its.*

Now and then, the lens affixed to his chest provides glimpses of the wound. The sight pulls at a nerve in the mind. The gory flashes of his hand is a reminder of the fragility of the human body, and that knowledge is felt as a cold, sickening, tremble in the gut.

Charlie is holding his damaged hand, as though it were an injured bird. Thick, crimson blood is dripping between his fingers. A flap of white flesh hangs down. It's not large but it's enough to elicit a gagging at the back of the throat.

This isn't something easily fixed. A distressed red, turning purple, blotch spreads across his stiff knuckles.

The camera rocks against his chest giving a shuddering, woozy view of the room. Charlie yanks open the first aid kit and stops yelling. The only noise is Richie wailing from the kitchen. The distance drowns its intensity down to a thin screech, and is lost altogether when the audio fills with a sharp intake of breath as peroxide pours over the mangled appendage. Stinging whiteness foams on the cut and blood spills onto the table next to piles of folded laundry. It pools along the edge and drips down to the new oak floorboards.

"Oh, geez." Mary tries to take the hand but he snatches it away from her. "We need to get you to a hospital."

"I'm okay. No hospitals."

"That," she says, pointing at his wound, "is not okay."

"I said, I'm fine." Charlie pulls a towel from the laundry pile and wraps the injury.

Richie is still sobbing in the background.

"Shut up." Charlie says and from the change in the camera angle, he must be on his tiptoes yelling over Mary's head to force his voice into the kitchen. "What are you crying about? You don't hear me crying. Next time I say stay out. Stay the fuck—"

The child's crying erupts into the howl of an animal in distress and drowns out the rest of Charlie's speech.

"He didn't mean it, Charlie." Mary has her hands against his chest.

And then there it is: Charlie turns from her. Two steps. One. Two. And he's facing the wall. His good hand makes a morbid red print as he steadies himself. Even with the fresh paint, the drywall greedily soaks up the blood.

"I know. I know. It just hurts like hell. I'm not thinking straight."

Mary comes around and gets in front of him. She's close enough that her old, red plaid work shirt takes up most of the frame. With Mary blocking the screen, it is possible to think the two of them move in unison and what happens next is only an illusion, except for the crook of her arm, which casts a shadow on the wall behind them.

The only light comes from the windows and it has a murky, underwater quality to it. The shadow is gray on gray, but it's distinct and it never moves or waivers.

"We have to go to the hospital." The steadiness of her plea highlights her fear.

"We can't afford another trip to the hospital." It's said with a catch in his throat. That break in his voice parallels the break in his spirit, and it's possible to feel sympathy for Charlie again. Here is a man cracking under stress. Although money and budget are never discussed on the tapes, constant clues point to the project not going as planned and bleeding them dry. "I'll patch myself up upstairs. I'll be fine. It's not as bad as it looks. Honest."

He steps past Mary. She's looking down and away from him, perhaps sullen from the realization their family cannot afford to repair themselves as well as their home.

He walks toward the foyer. Mary's shadow isn't on the interior wall anymore, but on the front wall next to the picture window. The light never changed but the room has. There is no logical way to explain it but the house is twisting and maneuvering around them.

6.

MIDNIGHT HAD COME AND GONE. The only light was from the computer monitor. Up close, it cast a white glow that bleached Molly's face. Farther out, it faded to a dim, flickering blue on the apartment walls. The only sound was from a bony tree branch squeaking as it drew patterns on the window with a restless finger.

For the second night in a row, Molly stayed up searching through videos tagged with the word *paranormal*.

Unlike the night before, Kevin wasn't in the next room snoring to the sounds of the basketball highlights on TV. He had stayed out after work, meeting some friends for drinks again. Molly wouldn't hear from him until he stumbled in. The beers he drank would shorten his already clipped temper.

TGIF.

Molly tried to focus on the peace Kevin's absence bought her, but knew it only delayed the inevitable confrontation when he came home and found her still working on her Garrison project.

He didn't understand that not everything was as mundane as accounting. Her work didn't have a neat, little schedule. She didn't get to put it aside and forget about it when the clock turned five or when the weekend rolled around. That was the difference between a calling and a job. But Kevin didn't want to hear about it. He wanted her to relax, stop taking it so seriously, spend her time on frivolous things — like he did.

Molly had too much work in front of her for that.

Searching out videos on the Internet was akin to going through a library book by book, hunting for a specific quote. Sorting through the postings to find relevant ones took up far more time than actually watching them. She dismissed more than three quarters of the videos without bothering to press play. Some had enough description to exclude them from any association with the Garrisons. Some were simply too old. Others were pornographic.

Most of the remaining ones, she shut off somewhere between the three- and fifteen-second mark. That was enough time to see the people and the location and realize there was nothing in the film to interest her.

A rare few, she watched to the end. So far, none were worth including in her case study.

Molly was close to dozing in her chair when she came across a posting from some teenager in Maine with the title *Roof Jump.* The blurb said: "This begins as a childish dare. But what happens at the end will leave you screaming."

Fat chance. Most of these "terrifying" videos were better categorized as silly. Or juvenile and disgusting. Molly was about to pass Roof Jump by, but the frozen image on the thumbnail stopped her. The picture was of a boy standing with trees behind him, there were no trunks, only thick summer foliage. Something in the deep, heavy green of leaves all around him and the complete lack of sky made Molly feel it might be worth three seconds of her time.

ROOF JUMP

A BOY OF MIDDLE-SCHOOL AGE stands on a roof. His face is a round, white moon with a smudge of grime on his cheek and a spray of freckles across his nose. A mop of greasy brown hair droops over his head. Around him there is nothing but trees. It's a dense wall of green. Not a sliver of sun or sky penetrates it. It's almost as if he's in a cave somewhere, in some subterranean trench where daylight has never touched — if trees grew underground.

"C'mon. You're the one who wanted to do this, Trev. Don't tell me you're chickening out." The person speaking is unseen, but a brightness of youth is in his voice. The prepubescent quality makes it almost indistinguishable from a girl's.

"The only chicken here is you. I'm getting warmed up, is all," Trev says.

"Well, get on with it. If my dad catches us doing this, I'm dead."

"All right." The boy stands up a bit straighter and looks into the camera. "You are about to witness one of the greatest feats of daring Pineview Lane has ever seen." He's not talking to the other boy but to an imaginary audience. "I, Trevor McDonald, will make history today by—"

"History? It's only three feet." The camera swivels down. The boys each stand on a different house. Between them is a gap descending two stories to a bare patch of scrubby dirt.

"No. It's seven or eight at least."

"Well, are you going to do it or not?"

"Here it goes." Without any further preamble, Trevor takes a three-step run and leaps across the gap. He passes the lens with a whoosh. The boys explode with hoots and laughter.

All that's seen is a blur of roofing tiles, trees, running shoes, and hands. Trevor applauds himself and the other boy is almost incoherent, giddy with the adventure.

He says, "You did it. I can't believe it. That was awesome." But it's sporadic and broken with croaks of laughter.

Trevor picks himself up and climbs across the pitch of the roof. The friend follows him with the lens pointed down at the shingles. The camera bounces with each step, forgotten, until Trevor says he's ready and it's raised to him. The view is swamped in green again. It's as though the leaves are a close ring of fog pressing in against the houses. Instead of the freedom of the outdoors, this feels tight, contained, suffocating.

The boys are now on the other side of the house. A gutter choked with dead leaves is a few steps behind Trevor's heels.

"All right," he says. "The incredible daredevil Trevor McDonald will now go for the roof-jumping record with one more mighty leap."

Feeling confident after his success, Trevor doesn't hesitate and takes off at once. He turns, vaults over to the next house, and lands on his hands and knees. He scrambles to his feet. Ta-da!

After a self-congratulatory pause in the action, he says, "Now it's your turn."

"Me? What?" The unseen boy clearly wasn't expecting to have to take part in this crazy game.

"You can't film me jumping to the next house if you're standing there. Can you? Besides, this is a short one. It's easy."

The unseen boy makes an awkward groan of hesitation. It's not loud but the mic is right by his mouth and captures everything, even if Trevor doesn't seem to hear.

"What's a-matter? Scared?" It's Trevor's turn to taunt.

"Am not. But I can't jump with the camera."

"Toss it. Don't worry. I'll catch it." He puts his hands out like he's waiting for a football.

The boy's nervousness comes across through a tremor in the footage. It's slight, barely a 2.5 Richter scale jitter, if you could measure the fine movements of a child's hands. But he accepts the dare and the image becomes a swirling madness as the camera spins end over end. Amid the bursts of charcoal and shadowy emerald are the first and only glimpses of a perfect blue sky, flashing between the darknesses.

The kaleidoscope of images stops with a jarring shudder. Things stabilize and Trevor aims the camera.

The image is almost exactly the same as the one at the beginning of the tape. Only it's a different roof and a different boy.

It's Henry Garrison. He's one or two years younger than Trevor. The older boy must be leveraging his age to manipulate him into mischief and danger. A bad influence, as a parent might say.

As Mary might say, if she were there. And in a way, she is.

Mary is vivid in her son's features. It has never been more evident this is her child. He has the same pronounced cheekbones and identical golden brown hair. Their eyes are the same light turquoise with a darker halo at the rim of the iris. Even the pout on his lip was borrowed from her face.

The boys go through a familiar rehash of trash talk. Only now, their roles are reversed. Henry looks over the edge. The expression on his face says that the distance he's measuring isn't from one roof to the other, but from his feet to the ground.

"C'mon already."

"Should we be doing this? I mean, it's not our house. What if the Willards catch us?"

Trevor lets out a brash laugh. "Don't be a baby. I double-dog dare you."

"Okay. Okay." Henry backs up until he's close to the roof's gentle peak.

He lopes down, his spindly legs pinwheeling wildly, building momentum. He reaches the edge and jumps. His light body flies across. He's over. His feet only have to touch the other roof.

Then, the inexplicable happens: he falls.

No. It's not a fall.

Even after countless times of rewinding and re-watching, the moment is the same: Henry is yanked out of the air and dragged backward into the gap, as though invisible hands have grabbed him — as though the house itself pulled him back toward it, refusing to let him leave.

His small hands scramble to gain a hold on the shingles and then the gutter, but the force that has hold of him is too strong and soon he vanishes beneath the roofline.

7.

THE RESTAURANT HAD THAT GENERIC, anywhere-in-America feeling Molly had forgotten existed. In the small college town where she had lived so long, the places were cheap and funky, brimming with character and individuality. There was never a reason to venture out to one of these chain restaurants, which popped up by the highways and in shopping malls.

But she had left her town and her apartment behind. She was in uncharted territory now. "New beginnings," she said to herself as she passed the hostess station.

Charlotte was at a table in the bar. A large flat-screen mounted in the corner played football recaps. The furnishings were dark mahogany and black leather. The lighting was all Edison bulbs in iron cages. It was a versatile space. Chic enough so singles could come here to sip martinis and cosmos and try to hook up; casual enough so married men could drink beer and eat chili fries while watching the game to avoid going home to their families. After the nearby offices closed for the day, it would be packed. But at lunch time, only the dining room was full of people, the bar area was all but deserted.

"Thanks for meeting me," she said to Charlotte before sitting down.

"Of course, dear. What's the matter?" Her sympathy was undercut by a note of impatience.

Annoyance bloomed in Molly's head. Was it such a bother to have lunch with her? Was Charlotte's time so valuable?

She put a clenched fist to her lips and counted to ten, forcing a slow, calming breath through her lungs. She wasn't being fair to Charlotte. Molly's nerves were raw. She'd woken up euphoric with her late-night discovery still fresh in mind, but after discussing it with Kevin, the elation had decayed into an impotent rage. Combined with her lack sleep, the emotions had left her teetering on the edge of control. She needed to remember Charlotte was doing her a favor meeting her today. She could have said no. She could have said she was too busy. Or she could have made Molly drive into the city instead of meeting her near the interstate.

When Molly felt calmer, she said, "I'm sorry. I'm at my wits end."

"You mentioned on the phone something about the family you were writing your paper on. Are you still working on that? I thought you'd be done with that silly thing by now."

Silly. Molly made an effort to look down at the menu and ignore her friend's choice of words. "It's still a work in progress. But that's not the problem. It's Kevin."

"Kevin?"

"Things haven't been going very well. I think it might be over between us."

"Is that what this trip is about? Are you leaving him?"

"No." There was so much Molly wanted to say. How could she compress everything that had happened, everything she had felt, into something that would make sense? Any attempt would be inadequate and fail to express the situation, so she simply said, "Not yet, anyway. He's changed."

"In what way?"

"He…" The words were fish passing her in a river. She tried to scoop the right ones out, but they wriggled from her fingers. "He's always against me. We fight all the time. He treats me like a child."

"That doesn't sound like Kevin. What do you fight about?"

"Everything." *Yes, they fought about everything*, Molly thought, feeling satisfaction at it being expressed so concretely.

He had become so controlling. It was as though something had snapped inside of him. Or perhaps he had only been biding his time, waiting for her to surrender to him, but he'd grown tired of waiting and decided to take steps to dominate her life. He wouldn't be happy until she dropped out of school, took some meaningless job, and spent her spare time cleaning the house and making dinner. The bastard wouldn't be satisfied until she gave up everything that was important to her. Not until she stopped wasting her time on her thesis and *The Garrison Project*, and *stopped acting like a crazy person*, as he put it.

Marriage to Kevin would be a prison. It would be a life of servitude where every time she tried to express her thoughts and dreams, he would shut her down and call her crazy.

"I'm so sorry to hear that. You two always seemed like the perfect couple." A flatness to Charlotte's statement negated its sentiment as though she had never believed it, as though she had always seen behind the sham of appearances to the imperfections hiding beneath. Or maybe Charlotte was thinking of her own flawed relationship. After years of public fights, on again off again status changes, and the not entirely successful glue of a child, perhaps she couldn't see this as anything other than inevitable.

Charlotte took a long sip of her drink and the silence amplified. She put the glass down too carefully, taking a moment to adjust the position of the straw before looking at Molly again. "So what are you going to do?"

"I don't know. We said we'd talk about it later. After we cooled down."

The lie was easier to face than the truth. It was easier to pretend they were still equal participants in their relationship. But there had been no agreement. Kevin had told her, "We'll discuss this when I get home," as he headed off to work that morning. As though Molly needed his permission to do things now. And worse, she hadn't argued with him. She had stared down at her feet sullenly as he stormed out. When the door closed, the shame set in. Molly should have stood up for herself.

Why were the things she wanted open to debate? He couldn't bully her around.

Except he could, and he had.

Alone in the apartment, Molly saw herself at a crossroads. She could either sit there meekly, waiting for Kevin to come home so she could make her case again and hope he'd allow her to go on her trip. Or she could stake her independence and go.

So, she packed her bag, got in the car, and left.

"I don't know what difference talking will make. We aren't the same people we used to be. It's almost like..." Molly bit her lip and held the open menu in both hands, creating a protective shield between her and the anticipated criticism. "No. You're going to think me silly."

"How long have we known each other? You can tell me anything."

The genuine concern in Charlotte's expression eased the fear she might take Kevin's side in this and leave Molly completely shut-out and alone.

Emboldened, she started to explain her thoughts. "I keep watching those tapes of the family and I see Kevin and myself in that couple." Charlotte's eyes narrowed and Molly glanced down to avoid them. She couldn't take any more disapproving looks. They would dissolve her courage like an acid bath. But Charlotte made an encouraging murmur and Molly went on, explaining how she saw little signs of the Garrisons' fractured relationship in the progression of the episodes. Sadness and hate could be read in the most casual of their words or gestures. Somehow Molly knew it would be the same with her and Kevin one day if something didn't change. It was heartbreaking seeing it unfold in this immutable time capsule. Molly was forced to watch this poor woman live out a tragedy and couldn't do anything to help. How many times watching the videos had she wished she would take the kids and leave him?

"Wait." Charlotte stopped her. "The woman in those tapes is also called Molly?"

"No." Molly looked at her friend, wondering why on Earth she'd ask such a thing. "Her name is Mary."

"You said *Molly.*"

"You must have misheard me. They do sound awfully alike now that you mention it." The two of them were awfully alike.

Charlotte watched her without saying anything, as though Molly was a stray dog whose temperament was unknown.

She truly was all alone. How come no one could understand the misery she felt? Molly's tears began to come again, and she pushed them back, swallowing them down until her pain was contained in a phlegmy lump in her throat.

"Anyway, enough of all this sad talk," she said, fixing her eyes on the white sheet paper-clipped to the menu with the day's special. *That's what I'll have. A special meal for a special day.* "I've made a breakthrough on my thesis. I found a tape posted by one of Henry's friends — not a very good friend, if you ask me. It was so horrible what happened to Henry, because of this boy. Such a bad influence. But I was able to figure out where the Garrisons lived from his online profile. So I'm going — I'm really going. I'm going to go see the house for myself."

Molly looked up, the tears forgotten. A smile beamed on her face so wide her cheeks hurt with a joy she hadn't felt since she was a child.

Charlotte's mouth was open in horror.

No one understood her anymore.

DAY 1: A DREAM HOUSE (PART ONE)

THERE HAS ALWAYS BEEN SOMETHING POIGNANT about the first episode. Of the entire collection, it is the least eventful but perhaps the saddest to watch. The digital frames have flickered by so many times it can be invoked entirely by memory.

It opens with the same cheap title graphics and stiff introductions, accompanied by some jarring, upbeat, synthesized theme music (which must have been grating even to the Garrisons, since it's dropped from the later episodes).

From the title sequence, it transitions to a montage of exterior shots, which begins with an image of the house from the distance. The band of pavement in the foreground suggests the camera is across the street in an empty field or a neighbor's yard. In voice-over, Mary finishes her introduction with, "…and welcome to our dream house."

Whatever you think of when you hear the phrase "dream house," this sad structure isn't it. The color is an uneven, weathered gray, which fades into its dull surroundings like camouflage. The doors and windows are arranged with the straightforward simplicity of a preschooler's drawing. Each floor has two symmetrical windows, all with four panes of glass. The door is centered between the bottom two. But a child probably wouldn't have included the screen door hanging on by the bottom hinge in her picture, or the trees that screen part of the façade and conceal most of the roof.

Nothing about the house appears sinister. This is no witch's cottage in the woods. It's simply post-war housing suffering from neglect. Squint and — yes — it's easy to see why Mary and Charlie are happy to have it, why it's their dream home. There is potential. It's a wreck but a young couple of limited means could make a life here.

The next shot is taken from much closer and the leap feels like a rapid zoom, blinked and missed. In this image, everything beyond the house disappears. There are no edges to escape from the mottled dirt covering the siding. At one time, it had been white but age and grime has wiped away its purity. The paint falls off in flakes like molting reptile scales, revealing rotting, black wood underneath.

Maybe something evil can be felt now. But would any foreboding exist if these tapes hadn't become a never-ending merry-go-round? If in the last episode watched, their youngest son hadn't disappeared?

When the scene cuts again, the camera is angled upward on the right-hand side of the house. Henry's bedroom window is at the top of the frame. Above it is a scar of missing black shingles. Whoever has the camera — possibly Charlie — is pressed in by trees and the neighbor's house. He's forced to stand too close and is unable to capture anything more than a fragment of the building. A fisheye lens might help him get the whole side in frame but it would also distort the reality of what is seen.

A few more of these jigsaw-piece views of the side flash by before there's a full shot of the back of the house. Weeds grow up over the basement windows. By the door lays a decrepit wooden platform, which at one time must have been someone's idea of a deck. It holds a rusted-out barbeque and a heap of dead leaves.

The back of the house lacks the order of the front. On the far right, a porch juts out. The door faces to the left and is next to the wide, off-center kitchen window. A smaller one sits a foot lower on the other side. Upstairs has the same lack of symmetry with three windows of various sizes and heights scattered across the floor. If a child painstakingly drew the front, a madman hastily sketched the back.

But there's no time to contemplate the logic of the arrangement before the camera is back at the front stoop. Mary and Charlie stand on it with their arms wrapped around each other's waist.

"I know, I know," Charlie says, as though he's talking to an old friend who's giving him a ribbing. "It looks like crap."

Mary bumps his hip with her small fist and her smile disappears. But her anger is unnatural. It's something scripted.

Charlie picks up his cue and says, "I mean, it looks like a real handyman's dream."

Placing a hand to the side of her mouth and leaning in as though she's about to tell a big secret, Mary says, "That's realtor speak for we've got our work cut out for us. But a little hard work never hurt anyone."

8.

A HUM GREW in Molly's body. Quiet at first, it began as an unsettling background noise, a buzzing of unseen flies around her nerve endings, but soon it rose in urgency to a fevered howl, and a desperate crowd inside her mind chanted, *run.*

Get away. You are not meant to be here. If you enter, you will never leave.

In front of her, the Garrisons' house stood cold and silent, with the unsettling presence of a dead animal by the side of the road. Molly was far enough from the car that if someone came out and chased her, she might not be able to reach its safety in time.

But who would chase her? No one was there. The door and windows were covered in plywood. A large sign said, "Do not enter." It had been a long time since anything lived within its four walls.

Caught between a hill and a steep ravine, Pineview Lane ran along a dwindling sliver of land, lined with dilapidated cottages. All the homes on the dead-end street were in need of repair, but only the Garrisons' was abandoned.

In the videos, it was summer and the thick canopy of leaves cloaked the house in eternal shade. Now there was nothing but bare branches. Millions of gray trunks, like steel bars, caged it in. The November sky added no cheer to the property and turned the bright blue exterior to the color of a muddy pond.

Fallen leaves covered the path in a thick mat. Brown and dry, they crunched beneath Molly's steps, summoning the thought of a swarm of beetles.

Molly's body told her, *run.* But how could she?

What would Kevin say?

She'd look so foolish sneaking off to this house and then never getting farther than the curb.

Sweeping her hair back as she contemplated her courage, the clamminess of her palm chilled her temple.

"I'm tired of being scared," she told no one. She headed down the path, steady but without any sign of hurry. The constant crackle of dead leaves filled her ears with a meditative mantra and drowned out every other sound, including the voice of her inner fears.

She would only look around, she promised herself. She wouldn't go inside. It wouldn't be possible. It was all boarded up. Then when Kevin asked, Molly could say, "I couldn't get in. I tried." She'd be able to tell him she hadn't been afraid.

At the end of the walkway, Molly's eyes traced the route the boys took over the rooftops. The first big leap was on the right. From there, they crossed over the slight slope to the peak, then to the side where the houses were so close they nearly touched.

Molly had wondered why the camera never showed the house from the left side. It had been omitted from the montage in the first episode and was never revealed in any of the subsequent outdoor scenes. Being here in person, the reason became obvious. There was no room to film. A person could touch both houses with their arms outstretched. Any footage taken on that side would be entirely in close-up.

Curiosity pushed Molly to explore that narrow passage as she circled around back. If the trip accomplished nothing else, it would fill in this one tiny gap in her knowledge of the home.

No longer out in the open, the light vanished. The earth between the houses was bare, black mud. Leaves avoided the spot. It reminded Molly of the hidden hallway from the tapes: dark, tight, and so much longer than she'd expected.

Where would this lead her?

It was an irrational thought. She could see the backyard up ahead. But Molly couldn't shake the feeling that it was an illusion and this path was taking her somewhere very far from where she had started.

Around the halfway point, at the spot where she judged Henry must have fallen, she stopped and knelt to examine the ground. Some lasting mark ought to be detectable. The accident should have left a physical impression as permanent as the one it had left on her mind.

But there was nothing.

What had happened to that poor boy? What had happened to the rest of them? The most disturbing part of the videos was not knowing their fate after Richie disappeared.

But had he actually disappeared?

People on the Internet thought so. But maybe he had only been playing and found a place to hide. Perhaps they'd located him a few minutes later in a closet or under the table. Mary would have scooped him up in her arms laughing, and they would have all gone out for ice-cream.

Or maybe Charlie found him. He wouldn't have laughed. Charlie would have been just like Kevin, serious and grim — tired of foolishness.

Stay hidden, Richie, Molly prayed. *Stay hidden.*

The dark was good and safe and you could stay there forever and nothing would ever hurt you. Molly thought of that darkness and longed to crawl into it and hide in its folds of protection, where no one would ever hurt her again.

She stepped into the backyard. After being in that dark walkway, the sky seemed too bright. But the light and the open space cleared her thoughts, as though an old wool blanket had been weighing her down— a rough and heavy one that smelled of mildew and moth balls — but with it shed, she felt lighter. Healthier.

Molly shook away the strange thoughts plaguing her. *Nobody hurts me.*

She rushed across the lawn, plowing through the piles of leaves. In another time and place, she might have enjoyed the simple game of kicking them about. Molly had always loved this time of year as a girl. The sun on her face and fresh air in her lungs almost made her forget the bleak visage of the house. But only almost. The cold shadow of the Garrison's home rekindled her fear and urged her feet through the yard with the goal of getting around the house and reaching the safety of her car.

The house was as forlorn in the back as it was in the front. The doors and windows were boarded up all along the main floor. Only the upper windows looked out at the world.

And one open basement window.

Someone must have forgotten to cover it. Or a mischievous person had pried the wood away to leave a wide-open hole so anything could crawl in.

The small, black gap stared at her.

It saw her.

That was how it felt: it saw her now.

It was like when she was in a hurry and would spot an old acquaintance on the street. At first, Molly would pretend not to see them, but once they spotted her, she knew it would be rude not to say hello and chat.

But you don't chat with a house. You enter a house.

Here was a chance to prove to everyone how brave she was. Here was a way in.

How could she run away after coming so far? That dark empty window would haunt her the entire drive home — it would taunt her with her fear and her foolishness.

Looking around to see if anyone was around — worried a neighbor would observe her, but hoping someone would stop her — Molly got down on her hands and knees and crawled backward through the window. She eased her legs in and then scraped her body against the uneven opening until she hung onto the sill with her fingers. They strained to hold her away from the fall awaiting her.

When Molly finally released, she was surprised the floor was only a few inches from her toes and didn't go fall away into an endless well.

She was finally inside.

DAY 1: A DREAM HOUSE (PART TWO)

NONE OF THE EIGHT EPISODES show any work being done on the exterior. The obvious assumption is they never get to it. Mary and Charlie never fix those cracked windows. Never tackle the landscaping and their big dreams of a play area, complete with a tree house and tire swing. Never paint the siding blue. ("I've always wanted a blue house," Mary says with bristling excitement when they're explaining all their plans. "There's just something so welcoming about a blue house.")

But read between the lines, and maybe that isn't true.

As they walk around the outside, they discuss contractors for the roof and the painting. They mention they might get someone to grade the yard so rain will flow away from the house and keep the basement dry. There are dead trees in need of cutting. And they want a new deck.

Could the dwindling finances hinted at in later episodes be due, at least in part, from the workmen they hired?

Nothing depicted on the tapes should cost enough to

create a household crisis, unless the budget was wildly unrealistic from the outset. But the house today is painted blue and has a weather-tight roof, which suggests much of the outer work was done.

So why were these jobs not filmed?

Is it because the focus of the series is on the work Mary and Charlie do themselves? Would showing painters, roofers, and landscapers be a distraction and dilute the show's appeal?

The answer is yes.

What makes *The Garrison Project* so endearing is the couple's very personal struggle to transform this wrecked house into their dream home.

And this is why watching Mary and Charlie going from room to room in the second half, on what Mary calls "the grand tour," is so emotional.

Something about seeing the house in its before state is inexplicably horrible. It's as though vandals have come and stripped out every trace of their hard work, scrubbing away all the very real blood, sweat, and tears that poured into the house's fibers.

But equally, and no less awful, is the constant reminder of the innocence with which Mary and Charlie enter this venture. Little do they know how their lives will shatter and decay with each fix and repair they make.

For the tour, they go from the foyer through the living room and the kitchen into the dining room, where the secret room and the demonic sigil still lay in wait. Then they return to the foyer and go up the stairs to visit all three bedrooms and the bathroom, only to end the episode back where it started, in the entryway.

They cheerily bid the viewers farewell "until next time" in the same pose as earlier, with their hands around each other's waists. Charlie has his back to the den and Mary has hers to the front door. The camera must be on a tripod in the living room. The afternoon sun comes in from the windows behind them, dimming their features and giving them a heavenly aura as bright as their dreams for the future.

In this first installment, their feet outline the mysterious sigil three times and keep returning to the same point. On the acetate sheets outlining their steps, the foyer is placed at the uppermost point on the G pattern and is a solid black blotch. If this house is a labyrinth, this is where the Minotaur resides. It is somehow the maze's entrance, exit, and epicenter in one.

9.

THE LAST WOOD STEP CREAKED as Molly took her weight off it. She thought, *I'm actually standing in Mary's foyer.*

The room was disappointing in person. On the tapes, it appeared to be a grand, welcoming space, but it was small and lightless with little to define it except for empty doorways leading off to other places. It urged a visitor to move on and discouraged lingering.

Mary had hung a chandelier resembling a colonial lantern here, but someone ripped it out and left only a tangle of hanging wires behind, so not even electricity could help disperse the murky darkness.

The living room had the same signs of abandonment. The furniture and tools were gone. Fixtures had been hastily torn out. A thick film of dust coated the built-in bookshelves flanking the fireplace.

Cracks in the boards covering the windows let in a whisper of daylight. It was nothing but a pale hint of illumination, but Molly's eyes had adjusted to the dark while traversing the basement, and it was enough to find her way through these rooms she was so familiar with.

The kitchen offered more of a feeling of home. The fridge and stove were gone but otherwise it was complete. The work the couple put into it remained: the island with its beautiful deep-grained wood, the hand-built cabinets, Mary's faucet. All of it was in place and ready to use. Someone could move right in.

Why hadn't anyone moved in here after they left?

It was fixed up so nicely. Surely someone would want this cozy, little home in the country.

Were people too afraid to live here?

That's silly, an inner voice chided her.

Molly had been silly when she first arrived, scaring herself with thoughts of ghosts and demons. More likely, she had been afraid of being saddened by what she'd find and fooled herself into thinking something about the place was ominous.

There was nothing to be frightened of. It would be such a lovely home. Molly could live here forever. Maybe she could convince Kevin to buy it and they could move.

No. She forced the fantasy out of her head. No future included him. She had to be strong and not give in to her childish hopes that things would work out.

Molly hurried into the dining room, taking quick steps, but the moment she entered, her feet froze in place.

This is where it had been.

Molly stared at the imaginary space in the center of the room — at the corridor that wasn't a corridor — at the place where the altar once stood.

She was so fixated on that spot she didn't even realize she was walking toward it, until she found herself standing inches from the wall. It was still the cheerful yellow Mary had painted it, just a little dulled by dust. A good cleaning and it would be as good as new.

Molly reached toward it. For some reason she had to feel the surface. Even if she was afraid, it was necessary. As though, if she didn't, the whole house might disappear and prove to be nothing but a figment of her imagination. Like a cottage in a fairy tale that vanished when you looked back at it.

This whole day had been like a fairy tale.

The words *touch it* echoed in her head.

With her hand hovering above the surface, the memory of Charlie placing his hand on the same spot came to mind. His masculine, blood-coated fingers superimposed over hers as her palm met the wall.

Upstairs, something moved. A floorboard creaked.

Pulling away, she called, "Hello? Is anyone there?"

Something that sounded like a child crying came from above.

"Richie?"

Could it be him? Could the little boy have been trapped here all these years?

Once the idea struck her, it seemed there could be no doubt: it was Richie. He had been waiting all this time for Molly to find him. He was trapped and scared but she would rescue and comfort him.

Yes. This is why she was here. The videos had led her to him. He had been hiding, but now they could be together. Molly and Ritchie could hide in this house from Charlie and Kevin forever.

Molly walked straight ahead into the foyer and raced up the stairs to his room.

She hesitated at the door, no longer so certain. Something was moving inside. The crying no longer sounded human.

What was waiting for her on the other side? Why was she here? What was she doing inside of this place? Bad things happened here. People got hurt. People disappeared.

Run, her body told her. From the sounds on the other side of the door, a mental image formed of a hideous ghoul with white slimy skin crawling on all fours and scrapping decrepit black nails against the floorboards.

Then the vision changed to Richie hurt and moaning for someone to come save him. She had to help.

Molly twisted the knob. She had opened the door only a few inches when the thing inside leapt out at her. It was so fast Molly barely had time to throw herself backward. She stumbled away from the creature, slamming against the door across the hall. The latch failed and the door fell away from her, sending Molly crashing onto the floor of the master bedroom.

She looked up in time to see an orange tom cat. It gave a hissing squawk and ran past her feet and down the stairs.

She'd gone and scared herself again. Molly shook her head embarrassed by her own behavior.

Mary and Charlie's bedroom was empty now. Not even a wire coat hanger had been left. The late afternoon sun was only a pale disk behind the clouds but after being so long without light, it was blinding. The two windows cast long frames of illumination, brightening the dark plum of the burgundy wallpaper into a rich scarlet.

Still shaking, Molly took a moment to collect herself before getting up.

The flooring she rested on was original pine, unlike the new hardwood downstairs. By her elbow the planks formed a distinct square, breaking the pattern of long lines stretching across the space. It appeared to be an access panel or a trap door.

Clambering to her hands and knees, Molly tried to pry it up. It moved but at the cost of a fingernail. A long strip of it tore off in the splinters, revealing the tender flesh beneath. Rubies of dark gore fell on the floor in scattered drops. She jammed her index finger into her mouth, sucking on it to soothe the pain and tasting the sourness of her own blood.

The panel stood open like a lid to a toy chest, revealing a dark gap less than a foot high. With her good hand, Molly reached in and fished around, still sucking on her bleeding wound.

Her fingers latched onto something and she pulled out a small plastic chip. "512 MB" could be read on the SD memory card. Last summer, Kevin had bought one for their digital camera with thirty times the capacity. It hadn't been expensive. Technology was always moving forward making them bigger and cheaper. It was possible this card had been in its hiding spot since the Garrisons lived here.

Molly slipped it into the pocket of her jeans and felt around the cavity to see if it held anything else.

She swept the back of the dusty compartment while the lid dug into her forearm. Something cold and hard brushed against her hand and her fingers crawled spider-like until they wrapped themselves around it.

Dread traveled from the object up through Molly's hand and filled her with a trembling chill. Her mind knew what it was by the feel alone, like she had held it before — like she knew she would find it here.

Charlie must have hidden it.

That horrible, sneaky man. After he found it, he kept it and stashed it away.

Molly pulled her hand out of the secret compartment, sitting back on the floor in a patch of silver light, and held the dagger from the altar up in front of her eyes.

DAY UNKNOWN: A FRAGMENTED FAMILY

THERE'S NO TITLE at the beginning. The tape jumps right into Mary and Charlie standing in the living room next to the fireplace.

"Hi, I'm Charlie Garrison." He smiles broadly while holding a plank of wood in the crook of his arm. It's almost as tall as he is.

"And I'm Mary." She forces a smile that falls short of her eyes. Instead of being a sign of happiness, it's a mask distorting the lower half of her face.

"Today we're going to build some shelving." He waits for Mary to say something, when she doesn't, he goes on. "Put some built-ins around the old fireplace. Not only will it add good, functional storage but it will give the place the craftsman style we're going for."

Charlie steps forward and pivots the camera to center it on a table saw. "Now, I've already cut most of the boards." Mary is static as the frame slides away from her, but before she's lost from sight, she sags against the mantle. "I just have this big guy…" Charlie pats the plank, "left to do, which should give you an idea of what goes into it. First, you're going to want to measure the length of the space, then measure the lumber." He runs a measuring tape down the side and lines up a pencil at the four-foot point. "And carefully mark it. Since this is going to be visible, running right under the window, I'm making sure to put the line on the underside. Remember, the graphite from a pencil can show through paint."

He places the board on the workbench. Uncomfortable silence hisses on the tape as he lines the machine up.

"Are you going to do something or do you plan on standing there and sulking?" The words seethe through his gritted teeth, while one eye peers over his shoulder toward Mary at the fireplace.

"What the hell do you want me to do?" There's no fight in her voice. There's no strength at all. The words might be defiant but they come across as a sign of resignation. "Just what the hell do you want?"

Charlie ignores the larger implications of her questions and pushes on with the show as though she's simply asking for direction. "I don't know. It's your design. Why don't you explain it? I'll chop out the dead air later."

Mary steps back into the scene with marionette movements. "Well, you see, they're shelves," she tells the viewer. She holds up a piece of paper with a grid-like drawing. Numbers and other notations cover it but they're too small to make out on the computer screen. Mary explains her inspiration came from a similar set of built-ins from a 1924 Batchelder catalog of designs. She goes on to detail the personal modifications they made in a voice devoid of emotion and inflection. Soon she's rambling as though she has forgotten how to stop the words from tumbling out. The phrase "integral to the character of the room" is used three times.

"Thanks, Mary," Charlie cuts her off. "I'm ready over here."

Mary stops talking mid-sentence and steps back, letting the shadows hide her features. Charlie puts his hand on the saw's handle and it whirls to life, but sputters to a stop before reaching full speed.

Henry has come into the room. He's facing his parents and the camera only sees him from behind. The tight stripes of the T-shirt he's wearing cause the video to blur, unable to capture the pattern in its pixels. His right arm is in a sling. Small scabs speck his left.

The saw's dying motor drowns out some of his words but it's easy to guess they are part of the plaintive mantra, "Mom. Mom." When the room is quiet and he has their attention, Henry says, "Can I go over to Trevor's?"

Mary says, "No, Henry. You stay home."

"I told you, I don't want you hanging around with that brat anymore."

"But he's my friend."

"He's a lying little bast—"

"Henry, go watch TV, baby."

"He shouldn't be watching TV. He should be outside getting fresh air."

"It's so boring. Trev is the only other kid on the street. What am I supposed to do if I can't play with him?"

"Go explore the woods."

"No! You stay close to home, Henry. I want you where I can see you."

"I used to play in the woods all the time when I was boy."

"Well, I don't think that's any ringing endorsement."
"What. The. Fuck is that supposed to mean?"

10.

MOLLY LEANED AGAINST THE STEERING WHEEL
and cried as the uncovered recordings continued to play on
her laptop. Alone at the side of road, no one around to
witness her sorrow, she was free to feel for these people who
she had never met without the risk of ridicule.

The strain of Ritchie's disappearance was undeniable.
The fissures that had existed all along were opening wide,
forming gulfs that could never be bridged. What was
witnessed in this series of fragments and half-episodes
wasn't a family but three lonely people, exiled in their grief;
their isolation working as an incubator, intensifying the
worst inside of them.

Had this process already begun with her and Kevin?

Even without the stimulus of tragedy, she felt alone.
Molly and Kevin had lived together but apart for weeks.
Their apartment was only two rooms but it might as well be
a drafty, abandoned mansion, inhabited by two ghosts too
ephemeral to share a human bond and barely aware of each
other's existence.

Could she go back to that now? Where else could she go?

Molly looked out on the deserted stretch of November roadway where the Garrisons used to live. She tried to gaze out past the horizon and into the future. Would a sign reveal itself to her? Would something point her in a direction?

She was still searching when the Garrisons called her back. The scenes had been running the whole time with jumpy cuts from one moment in time to another, but Molly had blocked them out without realizing it. While she tearfully wondered where she would go from here, the laptop's battery might as well have been dead and the screen blank, it was so far from her mind. But when the final installment began, it was impossible to ignore.

Perhaps it was the lurid red filling the screen. Perhaps it was the voice on the computer, which sounded as though it was talking to her.

"Hello again. I'm Charlie Garrison," it said. There was no sincerity to it, as though Charlie was lying. And considering what happened next, maybe he was.

THE GARRISON PROJECT: FINAL INSTALLMENT

AFTER A FLICKER OF BLACKNESS, the bedroom with the burgundy wallpaper and the two windows appears on the screen. The mattress is pushed up against the wall and the floor is scattered with lumber and tools. Charlie steps into frame.

"Hello, again. I'm Charlie Garrison," he says into the camera. He smiles in a way he hasn't since the earliest of the tapes. The corners of his mouth cut into his cheeks and lift his eyes. The irises shimmer the same blue as glacial lakes. He fidgets like a schoolboy standing in front of the class, forced into reading a book report. The hammer he holds never stops moving as though his hands don't want it but can't get rid of it. "And today I'm going to assemble the wall unit that will be our headboard. As we planned, this will be a major focal point to the room with built-in lighting and storage. I've already cut everything downstairs, so now—"

"What are you doing?" Mary's voice is dampened to a low mumble in the background.

"What did I just say?" His smile is gone, and the skin on his face draws back revealing an ugly, predatory scowl. "I'm finishing the bedroom. Somebody has to."

"What's the point, Charlie? Our boy is gone," Mary says, acknowledging for the first time on-camera the disappearance.

"You don't think I know that? It's killing me, but I'm not ready to curl up in a ball and quit. This is our home and I'm not going to sit around and mope like my life is over."

"This isn't a home. This place is hell."

"Don't say that." Cold fury fills his words. The tremor in Charlie's hands is almost too subtle to be picked up by the distant lens, but it's there in the shimmer of his taut, white knuckles.

"Nothing good has happened here. It's been nothing but hell."

"Hell. You call this hell? You do not know hell."

"My baby is gone, Charlie. He's gone. I can't stay here anymore."

"What are you saying?"

"I'm leaving. Henry and I are leaving." Footsteps creak on the floor, growing softer into the distance.

Charlie stands a moment. His face is as blank as a mannequin's. Life is restored to his features by something deep inside of him. It pulls at a nerve, causing his face to wince. Then he's running past the camera shouting: "No one is leaving. We're staying here. We are all staying here forever."

Off-screen, there's screaming and scuffling. Mary yells "No. No" repeatedly. Then Henry is heard saying, "Dad." It's a lament, filled with fear and resentment.

"How many times have I told you to mind your place?" Charlie says. At least, it must be Charlie. It doesn't sound like his voice. It's more of an inhuman growl filled with hysterical fury. It might not be him at all, but who else is in the house? Mary and Henry respond as one, bawling "stop it" over and over. A loud thump rings out and the camera's tripod shakes from the vibration.

Then, nothing is heard but a hideous beat of stunned silence. It's broken when Mary wails.

The shriek of anguish pierces through time and space. "Henry? Henry?" she pleads. The next words are spoken in the hiss and snarl of an animal protecting its young. "How could you? You monster. You horrible, horrible—" Mary is cut short with a cry of pain.

"A monster? Is that what you think," Charlie's speech is labored and he's breathing hard. "I'll show you how a monster acts. In fact, let's show the viewers at home how it's done."

Charlie comes back into frame hauling Mary by her hair. The hammer he had is missing. He drags Mary into the center of the room while she makes incoherent noises of distress.

"Watch closely," he tells the audience. "And always use the right tool for the job."

Charlie draws the ceremonial dagger from the back pocket of his jeans and runs the blade across Mary's neck in a smooth sweep, so quick the camera captures it as a blur. A line of blood opens and widens. He lets her go.

Mary drops, hands clutching her throat while making a terrible gurgling sound filled with desperation and panic. No one is there to help.

Charlie looks at the camera lens, hunching over as he leans in. "And that's all there is to it, folks."

Hostility and sadism transform his handsome face into a goblin's smirk. The smile is so strange and personal, it's as though it's meant only for the viewer — one particular viewer. It's transfixing and easy to focus only on his mouth and not look up at his eyes.

And it would be better not to look, because his eyes are nothing but two empty holes of darkness. They have no contour or gloss to them, only emptiness, like bottomless wells spiraling into the center of the Earth.

He flicks his tongue over the eerie grin and stares into the camera sucking all the light and color from the world beyond the computer screen. "They're all gone," Charlie says. "It's just you and me now, Molly. And we're going to be together forever."

11.

THE HIGHWAYS CUT DEEP SCARS through the New England hills with the pavement forming long trenches in the unending forest. Beyond the first rank of trees, the world fell away into a primordial night. A type of night unfelt since those early days of childhood, when a lamp made sleep come easier. But the headlights couldn't penetrate the wall of darkness and did nothing to dispel the fear.

The overwhelming night was the reason Molly found herself heading back home. How could she venture into the unknown when terrors lurked in the dark and when the dark extended so far? How could she continue on alone when demons, not only existed, but were chasing her?

As hard as it might be to believe, it was no longer Charlie Garrison by the end of those tapes. A dark entity had entered him.

Did it happen when he first discovered the altar? Or did it take place over time? Was his spirit eroded with every step he took along the paths of the house's choosing, as though the structure was some unholy prayer wheel designed to amplify evil?

But the whole family had walked in those patterns. Why had it picked him and not one of the others?

Because of all of them, Charlie was already corrupted. His anger had been the crack — the weakness it exploited. It crawled in through his temper and made him the tool to destroy the entire family. With each of his outbursts, it ate away at him a little more until there was nothing left of Charlie Garrison.

In those last few frames, had Molly seen the eyes of Hismael? How had the fiend known she'd watch it? How had it seen into the future and named her?

But it had been wrong. It didn't catch her. She had gotten away.

Molly had left Pineview Lane and that wretched house behind. It hadn't trapped her like it trapped the Garrisons.

She was on her way home. Even after all that had happened between her and Kevin, it was still the only place she felt safe. And right then, she needed to feel safe more than anything.

By the time Molly reached her street, the low fuel light was burning bright on the dash. She hadn't stopped the entire way. Not for gas, or food, or to relieve the strain on her bladder. Stopping would have been the same as inviting danger to find her. While she was moving, with the car doors locked, she had some protection, no matter how small. Even with the apartment in sight, Molly was filled with trepidation as she parked. The second she pulled the key from the ignition, she dashed from the car toward the warm glow of her building's lobby and up the four flights to her door.

Soon she found herself in her home and in Kevin's arms. His embrace enveloped her, squeezing her tight, making her feel safe at last.

"Thank God. I've been worried sick," he said. And then, "Where have you been? I've been trying to call you?"

"I went. I went to the house."

"I said not to go by yourself. Why didn't you wait?"

Molly drew away from his hug, which had grown uncomfortably warm. Something in his words itched, like a tag on a shirt scraping at the back of her neck. Somehow it didn't sound right, but she didn't understand why.

"Are you okay? Molly, are you hurt?" His hands pressed at the sides of her head and searched her face for some sign of damage. His palms burned against her icy skin.

Molly realized she wasn't answering. She was staring blankly like an idiot while he shouted questions at her. Finally, she managed to say, "I'm fine. Just tired and very hungry."

"Why don't we get you something to eat? We can go to the Bee and the Bonnet. Would you like that?"

With her head still in the cradle of his hands, Molly nodded.

"I'll get my jacket."

Kevin stepped away, leaving a void between her and the window. Outside, only a sheet of blackness could be seen. His words were still playing in her mind. *I said not to go by yourself.*

Isn't that how Charlie spoke?

He was always mentioning what he had said. *I told you… Didn't I say… How many times have I said…?*

MOLLY'S TESTIMONIAL

THE IRONY OF MOLLY BEING ON CAMERA is hard to escape. From the moment her pixelated eyes stare back on the screen, a peculiar connection to the Garrisons exists. She is now captured and stored in the same place they are. She has become one more file on the hard drive.

She is now another video ghost who can be summoned and watched over and over again.

The camera on her computer films her and the image has a fisheye quality to it. Her head fills the screen. The desk lamp makes her face glow and lets the rest of the room slip into darkness. She brushes a stray hair back across her scalp and glances around furtively before beginning to talk.

"It has been two days since I visited the Garrisons' house." Molly is whispering and it casts her voice into a lower register. "I thought I had escaped the evil contained in that place but it appears something has followed me home." She puts her hand to her mouth to stifle a laugh. It's not loud or long but there is a hysterical tension to it. "It reminds me of the *Haunted Mansion* ride my parents took me on when I was a little girl: '...and now a ghost will follow you home,' the ride said while a spectral figure sat next to me in the mirror. Only it wasn't a ghost that followed me this time."

The humor is gone from her face, replaced by a drawn, wide-eye paleness.

"It's Hismael. And maybe he didn't follow me. Maybe he was here all along. Perhaps watching the Garrisons' vlog released him from some digital haunted house. Kevin began to change around the time I started working on the project. Just like Charlie began to change when they started working on the renovations."

Molly looks over her shoulder as though she senses a presence. She gazes at length into the nothing behind her before returning to the camera.

"I think he suspects I know. He's been acting normal lately, pretending to be nice to me. Going through the same old routine to make me doubt myself. But two can play that game. I told him I've given up on *The Garrison Project* and threw out all the material I collected. This made him happy. Probably because the footage contains too many clues to his real identity. But I've stashed my notebooks in the trunk of the car and the videos are on my cloud drive. I keep the dagger in my purse, with me always."

She pulls the black leather bag up onto the desk and rummages through it. She grabs something, presumably the knife handle, and raises it an inch. The reflected sheen of the screen's light warps and reforms with the shifting contours of the purse. Molly doesn't seem to trust the camera enough to bring the knife out into the open.

"I'm afraid if I don't keep it near, he'll find it and use it on me. I will not die the way Mary did. I don't know where to turn but I can't stay here. I'm going to try to leave. Head out west somewhere and start over. But if I don't get away…if I die or disappear, this is my—"

"Molly?" A sleepy voice says as the doorway behind her grows brighter. From the weak glow, it is easy to imagine a bedside lamp has switched on. "Who are you talking to? It's three in the morning."

"No one, dear." Molly half rises from her chair, her head points over her shoulder as she reaches out to the computer. "I couldn't sleep. Must have been reading out loud without realizing it. No, don't get up. I'm coming back to bed."

Her finger meets its target and the tape ends.

12.

MOLLY STOPPED SHORT. The box she carried almost slipped from her grip. "Kevin, you're home early."

They stood less than two feet apart, both shocked to see the other at the front door. Kevin had swung it open as Molly reached for the knob.

"What's that?" He asked. "Where are you going?"

"Oh, this? Just some old stuff I was going to take to Goodwill."

He peered in the box, which hovered — trembled — beneath his nose. "Isn't that your good cashmere sweater?" Then he glanced past her at their living room. "Where's the computer? What's going on?"

Molly put the box down on the kitchen table. Ridding herself of it freed up her hands and gave her a moment to think without those terrible eyes boring into her.

There was no getting around Kevin while he stood in the doorway. Molly had to try to draw him inside and make a run for it. The last few boxes would have to be abandoned but it was a small price to pay. If she wasn't careful it could cost her a lot more.

"Look, Kevin, we should talk. You know things haven't been going well between us lately."

"What do you mean? I don't know that."

"Well, they haven't. They haven't at all."

"What's all this craziness, Molly?"

Every note in his voice strained with anger; the same anger that had engulfed Charlie Garrison in the end. He still hadn't moved. His hulking form filled the door. Molly kept her back to him. It wasn't the safest position but it prevented her from seeing his eyes. Eyes were called the windows to the soul but his only revealed a darkness, like the blackness that exists behind the stars. Kevin, her dear Kevin, was gone.

"I'm leaving," she said. Her hands clutched at her purse strap and she pulled the bag up onto the table in front of her.

"Molly, sit down. Can't we talk about it?" He moved closer and reached out for her.

"Don't." Molly pressed herself against the table to create some distance and rubbed her arms to fend off the chill of his presence. "I don't feel safe around you. I'm tired of your bullying."

"Bullying. What are you talking about, Molly? When have I ever…?"

The mistake had been in coming back. The trap was laid so cunningly she didn't see it until it was too late. She had run from the Garrisons' house all the way home and straight into the noose. If only she had stayed in the house. If only she'd never left.

"I shouldn't have come back."

"What the heck are you going on about? This has gone far enough. Sit down and we'll talk about this."

The two of them were reflected in the window against the backdrop of evening. They were nothing but wavering shadows playing on the glass. Kevin's body eclipsed hers. He seemed to have grown. Her head hid the bottom of his face. Somehow not being able to see his lips move made his voice sound disembodied and alien.

Molly stared into those eyes of darkness looking back at her from the glass.

"Molly." The demon gripped her by her shoulders and she felt the strength in its hands squeezing her, trapping her.

Was this how Mary felt in her final moments?

No. Poor Mary had never seen the warning signs. She had no idea what was coming. But Molly knew and she wouldn't be dragged down to the same fate.

Molly reached into her purse.

"Get away from me." She spun on him. Kevin's hazel eyes went wide and his face slackened at the suddenness of her outburst. He didn't notice the dagger until she drove it into his chest.

Kevin stumbled backward into the hallway, falling away from her. His hands went to the knife and scrambled to pull it out, while his momentum continued to carry him through the open front door. His mouth shaped the word "Why?" and his clear, terrified eyes pleaded with her.

The dagger came free and clattered to the ground, but he continued to retreat until he hit the stairs.

It wasn't a long fall to the third-floor landing, but when he reached it, his neck was twisted, and he didn't move anymore.

Molly was finally free.

13.

MOLLY STOPPED WRESTLING against the restraints holding her wrists when the detective entered. Composing her face, she pushed down the frenzied panic and feigned serenity.

"Ms. Heyworth, how are you this morning?" the old cop asked.

"All right. I would be better if I wasn't tied down," she said from her hospital bed.

"Doctor's orders. They say it's for your own protection."

Molly fought against the urge to snort at this. *Her protection?* How was she supposed to protect herself if she was strapped down?

"I think I would be a lot safer if I could move," Molly said, echoing the thought in her head.

The detective gave her a wan smile, as if to say *sorry but there's nothing I can do.* He sat down in the chair by the bed and draped his overcoat across his lap. The process of preparing his pen and a small notepad took long than it should have. The deliberate slowness of each movement sent the signal that he was in charge of the situation and they were going to have another talk, whether Molly wanted to or not.

The ability to walk out on a conversation was vastly underrated until it was lost.

"I've been looking into your story."

"Det. Stahl, it's not a *story*. It's the truth." Why did everyone insist on treating her like a child? If there was one thing she was an expert on it was stories. What she had told him and what she had signed as her official statement was no story. It was a chronological listing of facts.

"Sorry. I've been looking into your version of events." He rifled through his notes to find a particular page, as though he couldn't remember what he had come to ask.

"Now, you claim you used a ceremonial dagger, which you found in an abandoned house?" He waited until she nodded. "We've been having trouble locating the weapon. You stated it was left where it fell, but we've searched your apartment and your neighbors' and haven't come across anything matching the description you gave us. However, forensics did recover a kitchen knife that is consistent with the victim's wounds."

He was playing tricks. Tricks upon tricks. He was lying about not finding the dagger while subtly using language to undermine her.

"I'm the victim," she said, putting things in their proper perspective. "If I didn't do what I did, I would be dead right now, Det. Stahl."

"Of course. Poor choice of words. I should have said *the deceased*. And please call me Bill." Like using his miserable first name would do her any good. "Now in your statement, you mentioned the memory card from a camera that had evidence of other crimes: the murders of Mary and Henry Garrison?"

"Yes. It's gruesome, isn't it?"

"I wouldn't know. I haven't seen it. We haven't been able to find that either."

"It was in my pocket."

"We didn't find it with your clothes. Or in your home. Or in your car." He leaned forward and gave her a painfully earnest look, like a doctor about to deliver bad news. "We did manage to locate Mary Garrison. She's alive and well. Her and her family are currently residing in Portland."

More lies. She'd seen Mary die with her own eyes. The police were in on it. They must be. Had the demon gotten to them? Was it trying to get its revenge by incriminating her?

"Garrison must be a common name. I'm sure it was no problem for you to find a Mary Garrison somewhere. But detective, it can't be the same woman. You've made a mistake."

"I don't think so. I've read through your papers and everything lines up. It's the Mary Garrison from those tapes." He scratched at his gray hair and referred back to the notes. "Mother of Henry, Richard, and Alice — she just gave birth in August. Wife to Charles. Resided at 237 Pineview Lane until three years ago."

Stahl rested the pad on the knee of his brown suit. "I had a long conversation with her. It seems that shortly after those videos were recorded, her husband got a better job teaching at a high school in the city and they moved. Their son never went missing. There were some accidents but no violent episodes. As you might guess, she was surprised when I mentioned we had a woman in custody who claimed to have evidence of her death."

Even here, even now the demon was at work trying to confuse her. Trying to make Molly doubt herself.

Molly thrashed back and forth, shaking her head, denying his lies. It was all on the memory card. The card the police had so conveniently lost. Without those last hours of footage, a person could write the whole thing off. The public tapes only contained the weird altar and some minor mishaps. What those videos showed to the world hid the truth. The truth the police and this Det. Stahl were trying to bury like so many corpses. But she had seen the whole story.

What did this idiot hope? That she'd come to believe she imagined the whole thing? That she'd only dreamt she found the secret compartment in the floor? That she'd spent an hour crying in her car, alone with a laptop she'd forgotten to charge?

"No. Mary's dead. Charlie killed her because she wanted to be special and free. There was a demon in that house and it used his weaknesses to manipulate him. It made him kill her. Then it got into Kevin to hurt me. But it didn't work. I stopped him."

"I see." Det. Stahl got up and prepared to go.

"Don't leave me here." The strident undertone of a scream made her voice pierce through the antiseptic room. "What do you plan to do with me? What do you want?"

"I don't want anything from you, Ms. Heyworth. It'll be up to others to decide your future. When your doctor gives the okay, you are going to have a psychological evaluation. At that point, the District Attorney's office will decide whether to press charges or not."

"Charges? For what?"

"The homicide of Kevin O'Brien."

"I didn't kill Kevin." How could anyone think she was capable of hurting him? How dare they spread those lies? If she wasn't strapped down, she'd make sure this horrible detective never said it again. "Nothing could have ever made me hurt Kevin. It wasn't really him. He was already gone. Consumed by the demon."

"Right, I forgot, he was a demon," Stahl answered in a weary, flat voice, picking up his overcoat.

"Yes. Yes. Watch the tape I found. It proves it."

"There is no tape, Ms. Heyworth."

"It was self-defense. I would never have hurt my Kevin. I loved him. I loved him."

The panic that gnawed at her mind was that of an animal with its paw in a snare. Why was she always trapped? Why was she never free? Why was she always so scared?

Shhh, a voice in her head said. It cooed and made sounds to calm her. It was a voice so much like her own it was impossible to tell the difference. But because it was with her, she didn't need to be afraid ever again. It would protect her. And she would stay in the house it built for her forever and ever.

Acknowledgements

The book you are reading would never have been possible without the wonderful people at Wattpad. They, along with Paramount Pictures, very kindly asked me to write a short story as part of a promotional campaign for *Paranormal Activity: The Ghost Dimension.* That story formed the basis for this novella. I will never be able to fully express my gratitude to them for the opportunity. Not only was it thrilling and a huge confidence boost to get paid for my work and to be associated with such an iconic series, I also ended up with the bones of a story I couldn't stop thinking about.

Working on a book while holding down a full-time job eats into a lot of personal time, so I couldn't have done it without the support and understanding of my wife, Jen. I also need to thank the rest of my family, especially my mother, who never fails to ask about my writing and offers encouragement, even if she's far from a fan of the horror genre.

I would like to thank my friends and co-masochists Alys Arden and R.S. Kovach, who were also typing away furiously in the fall of 2015 on promo stories for Wattpad. The camaraderie I felt knowing I wasn't alone battling tight the deadlines was invaluable. And being included with such immensely talented writers, whose books I love, pushed me to write better than I would have otherwise.

I give a heartfelt thank you to Monica Kuebler for editing this book. I've been lucky enough to known Monica for a few years, but this was my first time working with her. I have no doubt this is a better book because of her hand in it. She saw past my myopia of word choices and kicked my favorite language crutches out from under me. Things every author needs on a continual basis.

Finally, I've been writing for five years now and I'm still awed that anyone would take time out of their lives to read my odd, little stories. So, to you, the reader, I offer my deepest gratitude.

About the Author

Born at midnight in a lonesome October, David J. Thirteen has always been attracted to the strange and otherworldly. His first foray into dark fiction was in high school, when he began writing short stories to entertain his friends. Fueled by his deep fascination with stories and storytelling, he has studied literature, mythology, filmmaking, and the media. Since 2012, David has been writing serial fiction on Wattpad, where he's published four novels. His first novel, MR. 8, reached the number one spot on the Mystery/Thriller hotlist and was featured by Wattpad, where it has received close to a million reads. It has since been published and is available for purchase worldwide.

David currently resides in Toronto, Canada and continues to write serial fiction every week.

For more information please visit:
www.DavidJThirteen.com